What in Life Were Wings

WHAT IN LIFE WERE WINGS

Barbara Isbister

This is a fictionalised account based on the war time experience of
the author's mother, incorporating historical events and the author's imagination.

Matador
Unit E2 Airfield Business Park,
Harrison Road, Market Harborough,
Leicestershire. LE16 7UL
Tel: 0116 2792299
Email: books@troubador.co.uk
Web: www.troubador.co.uk/matador
Twitter: @matadorbooks

ISBN 978 1803134 925

British Library Cataloguing in Publication Data.
A catalogue record for this book is available from the British Library.

Printed and bound in Great Britain by 4edge Limited
Typeset in 12pt Minion Pro by Troubador Publishing Ltd, Leicester, UK

Matador is an imprint of Troubador Publishing Ltd

For my mother, Zofia,

Kazimierz, Bryden and James.

*For all those who suffered and continue to suffer
as a result of war.*

What in life were wings
History may bring to heel.

Cyprian Norwid 1821-1883
The Mature Laurel

Man's inhumanity to man
Makes countless thousands mourn!

Robert Burns 1759-1796
Man was made to Mourn, 1784

Prologue

It is coal dark. I can hear the heavy breath of sleep from the huddled bodies on the floor.

Someone moves noiselessly like a smoky phantom, as we lurch from side to side.

The metal beast hisses and rumbles, jolting its cargo in and out of dreams into nightmares.

A shriek of torment pierces the night. Soulful wails for abandoned loved ones prick the air.

The imprisoned stench of urine and excrement chokes this windowless cell. My feet are wet where the pools of human waste have seeped in through my boots.

I don't know what day it is. I try to count the days and weeks I've been here.

Empty grey days merge into night. Time fades into a blurred stretch of shadow.

We are heading east. Where are they taking us? Why?

All I want is to be back home. To see Mother's eyes shining from the safe glow of the hearth, as she tells a story, Father smiling. Under their wing. I want to stroke Rex and feed the hens in the morning sunlight. But how…when, can we get back home?

It doesn't matter what day it is. It is somewhere around my sixteenth birthday. It could be today. Or maybe it was yesterday.

Part 1

The Beginning

Chapter 1

February 1940

The youngest angel is already asleep. His tiny chest barely rising and falling, like the petal of a sunflower ruffled by the faintest whisper of a breeze. The inquisitiveness of the other two, wide-eyed angels is helplessly disappearing against the unstoppable tide of sleep. Zosia [1] reads one more page, closes the book and watches them. How beautiful. How at peace they look. She kisses each one of them softly on the forehead and slips silently out of the room.

Hours later in the hush of night, half a mile from the farmstead, in the province of Lwów, a gunshot echoes through the hollow night. Zosia stirs in her bed but does not wake. A second shot and high-pitched screams pierce the depths of the fifteen-year-old's innocent sleep. Then marching. It sounds like hundreds of soldiers coming towards the house. The windows rattle with the thud of innumerable pairs of boots as they get nearer and nearer. The stamping cracks the frozen ground. Under her covers, Zosia is trembling and praying:

'Please, please, dear God, let them go past. Please don't let them come here.'

Orders are being shouted outside. The occupying Soviet soldiers, who have been in south-east Poland for the last five months, are on the road that runs past the front of the house. The stamping gets louder and louder. Close. Their steel-capped boots are grinding on the gritted path that leads to the front door. Closer. The marching stops. They are outside the door. She shudders. More orders. A familiar sound follows: the clanging of metal against metal as they cock their rifles and move them into position against the golden buttons and belt buckles on their military coats. They have done this many times in the past few months. The short, eerie silence stretches out like an eternity. A solitary bead of sweat trickles down her forehead, then another. The moment of silence is broken by more thudding footsteps, and an inescapable thunderous banging on the door. Her heart is thumping, punching against her ribs, like a wild animal fighting to burst out from her chest.

'Open up! Now!'

'It's alright. I'm going,' her brother Adam calls out, bounding down the stairs. There is more impatient banging on the door before he reaches it.

'Open up, immediately!'

Rex, her loving Golden Retriever, whimpers in the kitchen downstairs.

Zosia crouches at the top of the stairs and peers down through the bannisters. Adam opens the door. The long, slender neck of a Russian military rifle confronts him. Behind it stands a Soviet soldier with a thin-lipped grin, his eyes locked on Adam like a bird of prey.

'Hands above your head.'

There are more soldiers in the yard with rifles aiming at the front of the house.

'Everyone out and ready to leave in fifteen minutes!' barks the angular jaw of the soldier. 'Anyone who disobeys will be shot!'

The words reverberate through Zosia's head.

'What's happening? What is this?' says Adam. The soldier strikes him across the face with his gun. Adam staggers backwards, almost losing his balance. His hand is clutching his cheek. He looks at the soldier.

'What do you not understand? You will leave in fifteen minutes!' They all know enough Russian to understand the harsh orders.

Zosia trips over the hem of her long nightdress as she scrambles to her feet. She bangs her chin on the bannister rail, still disorientated from being woken in the middle of the night. From the top of the stairs, she sees Adam pressing a towel to his face. Blood is dripping from his cheek, staining the pale-coloured towel, and leaving a string of bright-red pearl-drops on the wooden floor, dispelling any doubts that this was real.

Chaos rips through the household like a raging forest fire. Her panic-stricken older sister, Genia and husband, Wojtek, desperately try to dress their three young children. The two of them are struggling to get their two-year old, Antoni, into his coat and boots, forcing his chubby feet into the boots despite his sleepy protestations. Zosia helps her nieces, Jozefa, seven years old, and Lucia, five, to button their coats, making sure they are wrapped up warmly and have not forgotten their scarves, hats and gloves. She throws on her own clothes at lightning speed, puts her small bag over her shoulder and grabs her shawl.

'Get some food from the larder,' Adam instructs his two younger brothers, rolling up a couple of blankets to take with them. Kazik and Leon do as they are told.

As Zosia follows the rest of her family out of the house, she glances at the old clock that belonged to her mother's mother, in pride of place on the mantelpiece above the dying embers in the fireplace. It is three o'clock, in the middle of the night, in the middle of winter. Her parents' black and white wedding photograph stands next to it. Their joyful, young faces, forever captured, smiling and looking lovingly at each other.

'Bye Mama, bye Papa, see you soon,' she says to herself, as she always does when she is leaving the house. It is one of the very few photographs they have of their parents, and treasured by all of them. 'If only you were here now.'

From the soldiers' flashlights, Zosia can make out the shadowy figures of about ten men. They look huge, their silhouettes even larger on the walls of the outbuildings. They are dressed in the familiar heavy, grey winter coats, their pointed, metal helmets gleaming. They all have rifles, four of them trained directly on the doorway of the house. Zosia's heart is still thumping. Just then, Rex brushes gently against her leg. It makes her jump. But the familiar touch of his warm, furry body helps to calm her a little.

More troops march past, down the road to the houses further on, where the same ordeal is being repeated, over and over. More villagers are being extracted and marched away from their homes by the soldiers.

None of them have had time to prepare. There has been no time to pack adequate provisions. No time to take any mementoes, keepsakes, or photographs, nothing concrete that can remind them of the family home and the time before that night, except what is etched in their hearts and minds. All of them are hoping there will be no need, they will be returning home soon.

The soldiers herd them with other helpless villagers, across the snow-blanketed fields and the two miles along the road into the central square of the village, prodding threateningly with their rifles anyone who slows or stumbles. Above their heads, Zosia sees a scattering of sparkling stars on the inky black parchment of the sky above her home, like studded diamonds in a distant coalface beyond reach. The icy wind smacks her face unrepentantly. The spindly, lower tendrils of the trees whip against her legs between the bottom of her coat and the top of her boots as she walks. Tears from the cold roll down her face and onto her lips. She licks her mouth and takes in the saltiness. Rex is still running alongside her, ever loyal. His soft brown eyes gaze at her for some spark of encouragement. She looks at him and pats him softly. They are marched across the frozen surface of the lake. A glint of light from the hazy, waning crescent of a moon reflects on a sliver of ice. Zosia remembers skating here, the gliding, sweeping motion and the invigoration she always felt. But now, without any skates, in the dark, she is slipping and losing her balance. Wojtek and her bothers take it in turns to carry Antoni who can walk but, not nearly fast enough to avoid arousing the attention of the soldiers. Jozefa holds onto her mother's hand and Lucia to Zosia's. They do as they are told, obediently, unquestioningly.

They walk in stunned silence. Zosia thinks how everything in her life has changed since the German invasion and the Russian occupation last September. During the five months the Russians have been there, they have been powerless against them. They have no weapons to speak of against the might of the occupying forces, who have established their authority, desecrating churches, destroying the cemeteries, and taking over everything they know. They are herded, but there is no good shepherd in sight.

They are marched through the centre of their village, Bortków and further on towards the railway station. There are hundreds of people at the station from the surrounding villages. Zosia recognizes some by sight and knows others by name. She cannot speak to any of them. There are no passenger trains, just some old cattle wagons.

The soldiers fire shots into the air. 'Get in,' they order, red-faced from the cold. Terrified, the crowds surge forward to get into the train. Zosia sees two boys, no more than ten or eleven years of age, break away. They are running from the train towards the houses and woods nearby for cover. The soldiers see them and immediately start shooting at them. The boys speed up. One of them loses his cap to reveal a head of thick curls. They continue running under the hail of bullets, but one by one they fall, dropping to the ground with a thud, like pheasants at a shoot. Anguished screams rise up from the boys' mothers who are watching helplessly, held back by their husbands.

Zosia and those around her are crying. Genia and Wojtek hide Antoni and Jozefa from the soldiers. Zosia shields Lucia inside her coat so she is out of sight.

'Anyone else want to stay behind?' says the soldier in charge. The soldiers have begun herding the terrified villagers towards the cattle trucks.

'Everyone in! Move!' they shout, firing more shots into the air. Panic-stricken, the crowd surges forwards, desperate to get into the wagons and away from the soldiers and their guns. Zosia suddenly realizes that Rex is still standing faithfully at her side. The soldiers will shoot him if they see him. She can't allow that to happen. She kneels down, hugs him tightly and kisses him on the head. She moves a few steps with him to where there is a gap between wagons and points at it, hoping that he will understand and somehow find his way back home. She strokes him and says her goodbye. He gives her one long, last, soulful look and obeys. He is gone.

But Zosia has no more time to think about Rex. The press of the crowd is sweeping her forwards, towards the waiting cattle trucks. A little way down the platform, she sees the familiar figure of her school teacher, Mrs Bienkowska with her young son, Leszek. They are being prodded along the platform by the soldiers. Mrs Bienkowska, always smart and in control at school, looks very different: lost, bewildered, her hair and clothes dishevelled. There are families of mothers and fathers, and their children, wailing from cold and shock. One youngster is holding onto his mother with his arms around her neck, and grinning inanely, in blissful ignorance of what is happening, as if he is expecting some great adventure.

They are being crammed indiscriminately into the cattle wagons. Genia, Wojtek, Jozefa and Antoni are in front, climbing in. Lucia and Zosia are following, Zosia is gripping her young niece's hand. They are being pushed towards the tightly packed wagon. It looks full. She has to stay with her sister and the rest of the family already inside. Zosia scoops Lucia up and passes her to Wojtek at the edge of the wagon. She climbs in behind her niece.

An elderly woman with a soft, round face, is squeezed up against the side of the wagon. She smiles at Zosia. Zosia manages a slight smile back, giving a small, respectful bow of her head. Genia is hugging Lucia who clings to her mother.

Zosia is one of the last to get into the wagon. She is pressed up against the side of the wagon, near the doors. She turns around to look for her brothers in the crowds on the platform. Leon and Kazik are not far behind and coming towards her. Adam is just behind them. People in the wagon will have to move in further to make room for them.

But as Leon is about to climb into the wagon, the three of them are stopped. They are showing their identification papers to the soldiers. They are all over eighteen, the military conscription age. Adam is twenty-eight. He has already completed his military service and is a qualified officer. Kazik, who is twenty-one, has completed his and Leon, only recently turned eighteen, is also kept in the group. They are not allowed into the wagon. Zosia protests to Genia and Wojtek:

13

'Please do something. Don't let them separate us.' Adam looks at them, the mark on his right cheek from the blow earlier that night is clearly visible. He signals silence. There is nothing any of them can do but watch in horror as they are marched off to different parts of the platform, Adam in one direction and Kazik and Leon together in the opposite direction.

'It'll be alright,' says Genia. 'They're just going to be in different wagons further up and down the train. We'll be able to see them when we stop…Don't worry Zosia, Adam will come and find us.'

Chapter 2

There are no seats in the wagons. There are no windows either. They are not intended for people but for transporting cattle and other livestock. There is just an empty, uninviting space. Just a bare, wooden floor. A dirty, wooden floor in a wagon that stinks of cattle urine and excrement. It has not been washed or cleaned out. There are bits of matted straw and dung on the floor.

About seventy to eighty people are packed into the wagon. There is not enough room for everyone to sit, so they take turns standing. About half of them have to stand at a time. The younger people stand for much longer to help the elderly, who sit on blankets or whatever they can use.

Zosia huddles with Jozefa and Lucia, shielding their eyes from the increasingly disturbing scenes outside. Screaming families are being torn apart, as young men are separated from their wives, children and mothers. By some fluke, Wojtek has succeeded in staying with his family, perhaps because he is older than her brothers and the standard army recruitment age.

Trying to edge further into the wagon with the girls, Zosia sees the elderly woman who smiled at her earlier. The woman has a few bundled belongings with her. She must have been given more time to get ready and collect a few things or perhaps she had known about what was happening, and she had supplies ready by her door. What a good idea. Zosia wishes that they had been more prepared and had brought something to eat and drink with them.

She looks around at the sad collection of frightened people. A tall, thin, old man nearby with sharp, pointed features looks haggard and grey. He is standing in the corner of the wagon, and staring out with lifeless, empty eyes. Zosia wonders what has happened to him. He seems to be resigned to his fate, whatever it is.

Genia and Wojtek have moved a little further into the wagon. He is standing, while Genia is sitting on the floor with Antoni on her lap. The parents are holding hands. Jozefa and Lucia are standing at their father's side holding on to him and on to Zosia. They have one of the blankets from home, which is wrapped around the two-year old, but there is no sign of the food they brought. There was no way her brothers could have passed it to them. What little Wojtek had, must have been lost, dropped somewhere on their way across the fields. Antoni is crying.

'Is it time for breakfast Mama?' says Lucia.

'Not yet, my darling.'

Without warning, the wagon doors are slid across and bolted shut on the outside. They fall into thick darkness. Lucia squeezes Zosia's hand tightly. Zosia puts her arm round her niece and feels Lucia's heart racing. She hugs her and tries to make her feel safe.

'Snuggle up to me and let's try to get some sleep.'

The train does not move for a long time. In the darkness and silence, a while later, Zosia feels Lucia's steady, rhythmic breathing against her own body. Lucia's hand drops by her side. She is fast asleep. Zosia wishes she had a blanket to cover her young niece. She uses her own shawl to cover her as best as she can. She doesn't want to think about where they are going or for how long.

After what seems like an hour or more, a soldier shouts his shrill orders. There is a sudden, sharp jolt as the train pulls away from the station. Lucia unaware, carries on sleeping.

The sun is just beginning to edge its way over the horizon, sending narrow, random shafts of light into the wagon. There is a crack in the wooden wall of the wagon where the clambering daylight breaks through. Zosia leans towards it and squints through it to see where the train is going. She sees the moving panoply of her life. The streets are silent, empty: no one walks, no market stalls, no village festivities, no familiar sounds of children laughing, singing and weaving their way back from school on many a long, soporific, sun-filled afternoon. They pass the town square, where just last summer she went with her friends to her first village dance, in what now seems like another world, an age ago. They pass the remains of the church where Genia and Wojtek were married and where both her parents' funerals took place and where they were buried amidst the now ravished tombstones of the once beautiful graveyard.

As the train gathers speed, they pass near their home, and by standing on tiptoe, she manages to catch a glimpse of her own house. In hope against hope, she strains to see if Rex has made it back. She listens for his bark. When will she see him again? When will she be back to feed him? What will he do till then?

'I'm hungry.' Lucia is awake and repeats her earlier plea. Jozefa looks up. They haven't eaten anything since the evening before.

'Oh, my darlings, I know you're hungry,' says their mother. 'We'll get some food as soon as the train stops.'

An old man and, what must be his grandson, are asleep on the floor next to them. The intermittent inhales and gurgles of the man's snoring distract Jozefa and Lucia. A few moments later, the elderly lady, who has been sitting on the floor nearby, leans towards Genia and with her hand outstretched over the sleeping man and boy, holds out a small package wrapped in a kitchen cloth.

'For you and the children,' she smiles.

It is the 10th of February, 1940.

Zosia knows the date all too well. The 10th of February was the day she had to complete her Literature homework essay and hand it in 'discretely' to her teacher, Pani (Mrs) Dziedzic. That meant without anyone seeing her, because Polish Literature had become a banned subject at school not long after the arrival of the Soviets in Poland. But she loved the works of Cyprian Norwid[1] and had written several essays about his poetry before the ban. She had been up late the night before finishing it off.

How could studying the poetry of a Polish writer be banned? And why? As well as that, history, and geography lessons were different. They were no longer about Poland. Religious education lessons had stopped altogether. There were some new teachers at school whose lessons were all in Russian. When she asked Adam about why the changes were happening, he had frowned.

'Because they want to wipe out our culture, our heritage, and most of all, of course, our religion. Everyone has to learn Russian, adults as well. They want us to forget our Polish roots, and become citizens of the Soviet Union.' He paused for a moment, as if he were wondering whether he should say anymore.

'I think what they'd really like to do is to remove all of us, all the Polish people[2] from here and make it part of the USSR, but that must never happen.'

Adam's ideas were unfamiliar to Zosia and shocked her deeply.

Her completed essay on Norwid's poetry was still lying on the kitchen table next to her satchel, ready to be taken to school that morning. Would anyone ever read it? Norwid's words were already echoing through her mind, 'I am homesick, Lord.'[3]

Zosia passes the first day in the cattle wagon standing in a tight space with Lucia and Juzia at the side of the wagon. Above her head, there are some freshly painted letters and numbers. They are Russian letters and numbers. Underneath them is some faded Polish lettering. She remembers other things Adam had said to her.

'The Soviets want to replace everything in our lives. They want to take over the schools, the churches, dictate what can and can't be taught, put an end to religious and community meetings.' She hadn't believed him, but he was right. Everything had changed.

But how had this happened? When had it all started to go wrong? In the darkness of the wagon, her little niece cradled in her arms, Zosia's mind slipped back to a day of unbroken azure sky and bright sunshine. September 1939. She was walking across the fields to the village to buy some food supplies for the family. Leon had come with her to help carry the groceries back.

In among the bales of corn stacked in the fields a couple of hares were running across the stubble. Trying not to frighten them away, Zosia and Leon crouched down in a section of uncut corn to watch the animals. The two hares were chasing each other, jumping in and out between the bales playfully. Then unexpectedly, the hares stopped dead. They rose up on their hind legs, and both of them were staring in the same direction, their noses twitching nervously and their large ears moving from left to right like antenna. Moments later Zosia and Leon heard it – a buzzing sound far in the distance. It grew louder. Very quickly it turned into a roar. It could only be a plane. But the sight of a plane was rare, there were almost never any planes flying there. Then it emerged from behind the trees, an airplane flying low overhead. They dived further into the corn for cover.

'Look, there's a red flag on the side of the plane,' said Leon. 'It's a Russian army plane.' It flew past, then returned. It seemed to be circling the area as if it was looking for something and then it disappeared from view. Neither of them had ever seen a plane like that before. What was it doing there?

When they reached the shop, Mr. Wisniewski served Zosia as usual, while Leon, who was pleased to have some time to read his book, waited outside.

'And, how's the family?' asked the kindhearted pharmacist and shopkeeper.

'Thank you, they are all well, and happy, now that the harvesting is almost finished, except for Jozefa, who has a bad cough. Genia asked if you have anything for it?'

He brought out a bottle of cough mixture. 'I can recommend this, one of my daughters, Sara, had the same and this cleared it up in no time.'

Zosia could still remember the very first time she ran errands for Genia. She must have been around the age of seven. Mr. Wisniewski shuffled around his well-ordered shelves, getting everything on the list Genia had made. Then he said:

'I think your sister's forgotten something very important.'

'Really, what is it?'

'There are no sweets on this list; no reward for you for doing the shopping.'

'But I only have enough money for what's on the list. Genia will be annoyed with me if I spend any of the money on sweets.'

'Well, don't you worry about that, let's see what we can do. Now, which sweets would you like?'

Zosia was taken aback, but it did not stop her pointing to the sweets she liked. He filled a paper bag with the chosen chocolates and fruit bonbons.

'There is no charge. What's the world coming to if I can't give a few sweets to my best customers.'

And since that time, even though she was now fifteen, he still put a few chosen sweets into a little bag for her. 'For you and for Genia's children,' he would say.

Leon helped her pack the groceries in the baskets they had brought with them. When they finished, they sat down on the bench in front of the shop, enjoying the warm caress of the last days of the summer sun. It was quiet, peaceful. There was no rush to get home. Genia had said that they should buy some lunch and have it before setting back. The smell of the freshly baked bread rolls they had bought was irresistible. They filled them with crumbly goat's cheese and juicy tomatoes. Then they had one sweet each, leaving the rest for their young nieces and nephew. They would set off in a short while, after Leon had finished his chapter.

The calm of their lunchtime was broken by three young villagers walking towards them talking loudly and gesticulating. It was Kamil, Janek and Szymon. They seemed to be arguing about something. Mr. Wisniewski came out of the shop.

'Is everything alright? What's all the noise?' he said.

As they got nearer, Zosia could hear what they were saying:

'War, it's war, Germany has invaded the west of Poland. Look at this.' Reaching the shop, Kamil opened out the newspaper he was holding and read out the headline:

'Germany Attacks Poland without any Declaration of War.'[4.1]

He continued to read, 'In the early hours of the morning of 1st September 1939, German troops invaded Western Poland. The Nazis are bombing Warsaw without any warning.'

'Did you see the plane?' said Szymon.

'Yes,' said Mr. Wisniewski.

'It's the Russians coming to defend us from the Germans,' said Janek.

'War! Bombing Warsaw,' the words screamed through her. Zosia could not move, trapped like a fossil in those seconds. Everything seemed to stop. She tried to make sense of what they were saying. She could not believe what she had just heard.

'Quick, go home. Get back to your families,' said Mr. Wisniewski. 'Tell them what's happening!' Zosia and Leon started running home as fast as they could.

When they arrived, Genia, Wojtek and Adam were sat round the table. Their grave expressions showed that they already knew. They had heard the shocking news on the wireless.

'We saw a Russian plane flying over on the way into Bortków,' said Leon. 'There was a red flag on the side of the plane. It was circling, as if it was looking for something or surveying the area.'

'What are they up to?' said Adam.

'Janek told us that they are coming to defend us from the Germans,' said Leon.

The days that followed were filled with talk of little else other than the news of war, when the young children were not there. Zosia tried to come to terms with the unimaginable situation that their country was 'at war'. She tried to understand what that could mean. The horror was slowly beginning to sink in.

A few days later, on the 3rd September, the news that Britain had declared war on Germany was on the airwaves. The front page of the newspaper on the kitchen table bore the headline:

'World at War over Poland.' Many countries, including Britain and France, were joining forces to fight against the German invasion.

Every day they listened to the wireless and followed the reporting in the newspapers. Warsaw was being relentlessly bombed over and over again throughout the month of September by the German Luftwaffe. The papers reported that between twenty to twenty-five thousand civilians had been killed and about half of the city's buildings had been destroyed. Finally, on the 26th September, Warsaw surrendered. The Germans took over the capital the next day. Mr. Wisniewski's great aunt lived in Warsaw and he was waiting to hear from her.

Bortków was a long way from Warsaw and from the fighting in the west. But on the 17th of September, Russian troops crossed the eastern borders of Poland. The newspapers reported that the Russians were coming to protect Poland from the German invaders.

'Reds Invade Poland. Russians cross border to protect minorities.' [4.2]

The adults talked about almost nothing else, but they themselves were unsure about what was really happening. The news was confusing. Zosia's mind was a tangle of information. There were reports that the Germans were transporting Jewish people to camps, that three million Polish Jews were fleeing. The Russians were taking over in the east of the country, claiming to be helping minorities and protecting the Poles, but they were destroying buildings and enforcing curfews. Posters were going up everywhere, stating that they had come, 'to extend the hand of brotherly assistance... to bring the Polish peoples out of the misery into which they have been plunged.' [4.3] Above the words on the posters, a large picture of a man smiled out. His name was Stalin.

Now, on the train, almost everyone is asleep from the exhaustion of the night's ordeal. In the dreadful cattle wagons, moving east, the events of the last months are spinning round in her head. She tries to piece together everything that has been happening and make some sense of it all. Why were they treating them like animals, threatening them at gun point and forcing them out of their homes in the middle of the night without warning? Why did they kill two defenseless boys? None of it made any sense. Was this really the only way the Russians could save them from the German invaders? Or was there another plan? Was what Adam had said, the real purpose? To remove them from Poland, to make it part of the Soviet Union? Was the unthinkable really possible? Was Poland being invaded by Germany and Russia at the same time?

Why hadn't the Russian soldiers just shot them all in Poland and left them there? Where were they taking them and why?

Part 2

Before and After I

Chapter 1

There are no toilets for them to use. Perhaps somewhere further down the train there is one for the driver and their jailers, the Russian soldiers, but not for the human cargo. There is no passageway connecting the wagons. They are shut in the wagon. The only exit is through the main doors which are bolted from outside.

'Do it on the floor!' snaps the soldier and laughs. They provide one bucket for everyone in the wagon. Genia weaves through the tight maze of captives with Jozefa and Lucia wriggling through any tiny gaps behind her. The bucket is already overflowing. There is nowhere to empty it until the train stops and the doors are opened. Until then, the floor is awash with human excrement and urine. There is no alternative but to stand in it. The strong stench and the soaking floor are inescapable. When they return, Jozefa complains that the hem of her coat is wet and stained. Wojtek will use his coat to shield Genia and the children from any further embarrassment and indignity of the bucket.

The old lady who smiled at Zosia when she was getting on the train, is fidgeting and not smiling now. She looks worried. She appears to be on her own. Zosia squeezes past the woman with the grinning child towards the elderly lady.

'Hello, I'm Zosia. Are you alright?'

'Helena Kwiatkowska,' she says with a small smile.

'Do you need some help?'

Zosia takes off the large shawl she is wearing round her shoulders, and opens it up. She holds out her hand and points at the shawl, offering to use it to screen Helena, to maintain her privacy and self-respect.

'Thank you, you are kind. I'm far too old for all this.'

Later Helena tells Zosia that she is a widow, and that her two grown-up sons were separated from her at the start of the journey, so she is alone on the train.

'You're not alone now,' says Zosia.

Amidst the misery and degradation, the initial embarrassment gives way to indifference. When the train stops for the first time and the doors are finally unlocked, they are given just a few minutes to clean out the mess. All they can do is empty the bucket and try to clean the floor with whatever can be spared. But it is still wet and stinks. There is not enough time to clean it properly and even if there had been, there is no warm sunlight to help dry it out. The doors are bolted again and the train leaves. They cannot lie down and sleep there.

One of the old men has an idea. A hole in the floor

of the wagon would solve some of the problems. He elbows his way through the crowd to a corner of the wagon, then pushing some people back from the walls, he starts stamping on the wooden floor to break it, but he is too weak. Others join in, taking it in turns to help. Wojtek, Genia and Zosia join in, all stamping on the wagon floor in the same spot, and after not too long, the goal is achieved. At least now all the waste can be disposed of onto the tracks and the constant stench can be alleviated. Everyone helps to clean up and dry the floor with whatever they have left: blankets, bits of clothing they can spare and they throw them all out through the hole. Genia and Zosia attach her shawl to the wooden slats either side of the hole as best they can, to create a makeshift curtain across the corner of the wagon, above the hole in the floor. Now there is some civility. Now the old and frail can lie down and rest. Now some of them can get some sleep on a floor as clean and dry as they can make it. But now it is even colder in the wagon, not only because of the hole in the corner, but because as Wojtek has noticed, they are heading further and further north.

When the doors of the wagon are next unbolted, they are all able to get off for the very first time. Zosia's eyes adapt quickly to the blinding snow and the dazzling sunlight in the blue sky. She takes several deep breaths, relishing the fresh air. Glad of the relief from the dark claustrophobia of the wagon, she helps Helena get down from the train, so that she too can escape their cell for a time. But Zosia is preoccupied. Now is the time she has to find her brothers.

Hundreds of people are running down the side of the tracks in both directions to the front and rear of the train, desperately scouring the long line of wagons for separated family members.

'You go that way Zosia,' says Genia pointing to the end of the train. 'I'll go to the front.'

Zosia remembers that Leon and Kazik were taken to the front and Adam to the back, but they could be anywhere on the train.

Wojtek stays with the children for fear they may be crushed in the crowds.

'Look for my sons too,' says Helena. 'Rafal and Zygmunt. I'll wait here.' Helena sits on the ground, too weak to move.

'I will,' says Zosia.

The cacophony of voices is deafening. Like a pack of screeching seagulls following a catch-loaded fishing boat, they are all shouting out the names of lost relatives, the wind flapping their ragged clothes like broken wings, as they race in desperation along the length of the train trying to find them. Zosia is in the tumult. But she can only see women, children and elderly men coming out of the wagons. Perhaps they are still inside further down the train. Her heart is beating faster and faster as she runs along the tracks, hoping to find them in one of the wagons right at the end of the long train as Genia had thought they would be. She shouts their names over and over. She can't see any young men at all. Not her brothers, not Helena's sons, none. She reaches the end of the train.

Clinging on to the shred of hope, that they must be at the front, she starts running. Genia is running towards her, throwing her hands up in dismay. She has not found them either. The tiny trace of hope has been ripped away from her. The thought that none of her brothers are on the train, burns right through her. Her throat is dry. She cannot speak. Unanswered questions fill her mind. 'Where are they?' 'Why aren't they here?'

She sees Helena coming towards her with eyes full of tears. She already knows the bad news. Zosia hugs her tightly. With her arm around her, both of them crying, she helps Helena get back on to the train. The sound of weeping can be heard in the wagon, followed by inconsolable silence.

The doors are bolted and the train pulls away. Zosia is curled up in the darkness of the wagon. Her family and Helena are next to her. No one speaks. She tries to come to terms with what has just happened. Her last question is the most disturbing. She cannot understand why the young men are not there. What possible reason could there be? But they must be safe. Why else would they separate military aged men, and Adam, an officer? They must have some plans in mind for them. She cannot imagine anything happening to Leon, Kazik and to Adam, her dear, eldest brother.

They must be safe. It is nothing more sinister than that. Nothing can harm her brothers. They must be safe. Were they on another train?

Many years earlier, when Zosia was about six years old, Adam had returned from a trip to the city of Lwów. He had been for a meeting with the family solicitor, travelling the fifty or so miles by train. When he returned, Zosia and Leon wanted to hear about his trip.

'Well, imagine the longest train journey you've ever been on,' he said.

But neither of them had ever been on a train journey of any length.

'Imagine the carriages: the smell of upholstered, leather seats and freshly varnished wood; the noise of the guard's whistle, the clatter of people and luggage on the platform, mounds of steam streaming past the window; the smartly-dressed passengers, the polite conversations with strangers.'

Zosia's eyes widened.

He continued: 'You can look forward to seeing places along the way and to arriving at your destination. The incessant humming of the tracks lulls you into a hypnotic daze as you sink back into your comfortable seat and gaze out of the window.'

Eager to hear about his journey, her face beamed.

'What did you see?' said Zosia.

'On such a journey, the view outside your window unfolds. It's like an art gallery, with an ever-changing display of landscape paintings: rugged mountains, deep, mirror lakes, a patchwork of green and yellow fields. All spreading themselves before your eyes like scrolls of scrupulously sketched parchment unfurling in the softest of breezes. Other scenes are of towns and cities, full of buildings and impersonal streets without end, interrupted by the sight of the spires and domes of a magnificent cathedral and the towering turrets of a majestic palace.'

Zosia did not understand all the words that Adam used, but she was captivated.

'And, if you tire of this, you may be able to have interesting conversations with your fellow passengers. Or you can read or play games to occupy your mind and help the journey time pass in a stimulating way.'

His words had made a strong impression on her. She hoped that one day she would be able to go on such a journey.

But now, sitting on the cramped floor in a wagon for livestock, the contrast was great. There were no unfolding views that any of them could easily see and enjoy. There were no comforts. They did not even have the most basic human facilities. The shell-shocked passengers were not entering into polite conversation. Survival was uppermost. And worst of all, unanswered questions hung over them: Where are they taking us? and why?

The time since they had left home felt like his journey multiplied by a thousand, thousand times. They had been on the train for weeks. They could not gaze out of any windows. There were none. There were no views to inspire the heart, capture the imagination or intrigue the mind, only what they could occasionally glimpse through the gaps in the wooden slats of the wagon.

The dark wagons were meant for animals, but they were being treated worse than animals. Animals would have been fed and watered regularly, and would have had their wagons cleaned out. But they had very little food and water. Nothing was cleaned out, except what they could manage to do themselves. All human dignity had been stripped away.

They had nothing with them to help pass the time except what was inside their heads, and that was becoming a more and more frightening place to go. Throughout the night and day, there was no escape from the disturbing cries and screams of children and adults.

Chapter 2

Juzia and Lucia's eyes are sparkling, Antoni is smiling. They are sitting huddled together, wrapped in the only blanket the family has to keep warm. The children are listening to Wojtek who is telling them a story. At least they look happy for a moment. A tiny jewel shining in the wreckage of a tarnished, broken bracelet.

All around, the sorry sight of bewildered-looking people, lost, far from home, who knows where. A low, murmuring sound in the wagon is growing louder and louder. Zosia looks round to see where it is coming from. It is the thin, haggard-looking man with the soulless eyes that she noticed on the first day of the journey. He looks so forlorn. He is sitting on the floor of the wagon, rocking back and forth, endlessly muttering the same words:

'Urszula, Urszula, forgive me. Can you ever forgive me? Please forgive me.'

The poor man is extremely troubled. What has happened to make him so dejected? Some of the passengers are kind and speak to him. Those less sympathetic, tell him bluntly, to be quiet, things are bad enough in the wagon without his droning. Zosia hears Wojtek telling Genia that his concern about the man is increasing. He is worried about the effect on the children who can see and hear the man's distress. He will try to speak to him. Wojtek edges past several passengers, moving closer towards the man.

'Are you alright? Can I help you?'

The man looks up and stares at him blankly.

'Juzia,' Lucia calls Jozefa by her nickname, 'Shall we play the 'Guess the animal' game?' Juzia nods.

'I'll start,' says Lucia. 'My animal has four legs.'

'That's not a proper clue, most animals have four legs,' Juzia says to her younger sister.

'Ok, here's another one. It has two legs and it flies.'

'A bird?'

'Yes, but what bird?'

I don't know. You'll have to give me some more clues.'

'Well, it's big and it's white, and it has a long, pointed beak,' says Lucia.

'Is it a stork?'

'Yes. It's your turn.'

Despite the man's lack of response, Wojtek tries again:

'I'm Wojtek, from Bortków. Where are you from?'

A long pause follows. Eventually, he replies, 'Władysław… Lwów.'

'My cousin lives in Lwów. I've been there a number of times to visit him. It's a lovely city.'

Silence follows. Wojtek says:

'I love the old town, the churches, the Cathedral and the Castle ruins.'

Władysław lets out a deep sigh and puts his head in his hands. A longer pause follows.

'We were married in the Cathedral, Urszula and I, forty-five years ago. My beautiful Urszula.'

'That's a very long time.'

'But now she's gone.' Tears fall helplessly down his face like the unstoppable flow of water over a cliff edge. He repeats his mantra.

'I'm so sorry,' says Wojtek.

'I should be with her. We promised each other. We made a pact. She couldn't bear the threat of imprisonment or deportation. We made a suicide pact,… to do it together.'

The girls are within earshot. Genia is tending to Antoni. Wojtek catches Zosia's eye and signals for her to move away with Juzia and Lucia.

'I couldn't do it, I just couldn't,' Władysław continues. 'But by the time I realised that, it was too late. My darling Urszula was dying on the floor. I held her in my arms. She looked into my eyes as the last breath left her body.' He weeps.

Wojtek puts his hand on Władysław's shoulder and squeezes it. Władysław stretches out his arms and hugs Wojtek.

Others standing or sitting on the floor nearby are silent as they too have become unwitting witnesses to his heart-breaking story.

Zosia looks down. She has managed to shuffle away with the girls.

But Juzia turns to Zosia and asks:

'What does 'suicide' mean, and what is a 'suicide pact'?'

Zosia is still in shock from Władysław's story.

'I'm not sure,' she says. It is not a lie. She has never heard the words spoken, though she is able to make a good guess.

Lucia is drawing and not paying any attention to what is going on around her.

'Aunty Zosia, can you give us another animal?'

Zosia swallows and takes a deep breath.

'Yes, of course I can, Lucia.' She hugs her niece and remembers a picture in one of Lucia's books back home.

'Ok, it has four legs, it's fat and loves water,'

'Is it an elephant?' says Lucia.

'No. Another clue, it loves sitting in water.' Will she remember the picture?

'Is it a hippopotamus?'

'Yes, that's right. Now it's your turn, Lucia.'

But there was another unfamiliar word that Władysław had said. It stood out in Zosia's mind: 'deportation.'

Some of the passengers are talking about Władysław's and Urszula's story. They have heard similar stories. Some of them knew people who could not accept what was happening, who could not accept being taken prisoner by the Germans or being deported to the 'frozen north' by the Russians. They saw no way out. Tragically, in the depths of despair, they took their own lives to avoid what they saw as inescapable threats. Stories of suicides spread.

Now Zosia was sure what 'suicide' meant. But she could not imagine that they felt so strongly, that death was the only solution. How could anyone choose to die?

Władysław and Urszula agreed to do it together. They had been married for forty-five years. That was three times as long as she had been alive. Her own parents had been married for nineteen, almost twenty years. The image of her parents' wedding photograph flashes into her mind. Their young, loving faces smiling at each other. They are smiling and looking at her now. They seem to be saying something to her.

'Our dearest Zosia, never forget, we love you more than ever. Don't be afraid. This will all pass. Remember, we love you more than anything in the world.'

'I love you too, Mama and Papa. I miss you so much.'

She feels guilty for questioning why they weren't helping her. She is comforted knowing that they are with her all the time. There is an unbreakable bond between them.

Later Zosia asks Genia.

'Why did all these people on the train just obey the Russian soldiers and leave their homes? Those who knew what might happen, why didn't they try to hide or escape?'

'There was no choice,' says her sister. 'You saw what happened when Adam just asked a question. The soldiers were terrifying, merciless. They were ready to shoot anyone who did not obey and there was no doubt at all that they would kill in cold blood without any hesitation. We couldn't take any risks. You saw what happened to those who did. We had no choice but to obey.'

For the time being, Zosia is partly satisfied.

But it was not clear. The NKVD, [1] the Soviet Secret Police said that they had come to Poland to save people from the Germans who had invaded western Poland and were committing atrocities there. Many seemed to believe this. She heard people on the train saying that they had seen locals throwing fruit and flowers at the marching Russian troops, in thanksgiving, waving and cheering them on. Others said it was propaganda and they did not believe what the NKVD were telling them.

Chapter 3

They are given very little food on the journey, just three, sometimes four loaves of bread per wagon for the whole day between seventy to eighty people. That is one loaf between seventeen at best, twenty-six at worst, per day. A small piece of bread, less than half a slice each for the whole day. They share it out between themselves. Once a day they get a cup of boiled water, which is supposed to be tea, called '*kipyatok*'. Nothing more.

At the start of the journey, Helena generously shared out the food she had brought with everyone around her. She had a few portions of ham and sliced sausage meat, a couple of homemade buns and a small loaf of bread. She gave most of it to Genia for Juzia, Lucia and Antoni. 'Thank you '*Babcia*', (Grandma) said Juzia politely. Lucia echoed her sister. Helena's soft face crinkled into a smile. She seemed touched that the girls had called her '*Babcia*' and from that day, all three children called her '*Babcia* Helena'.

She made sure everyone around her, including Władysław, got something. He was visibly moved by her act of selfless kindness. Any food that others had brought with them from home was also shared with their fellow captives. But within one day, it was all gone. From then on, they would have to rely on what the soldiers gave them.

The children are hungry. Everyone is hungry, all the time. The meagre servings of bread and water are nowhere near enough for the number of people. By the end of two weeks, many are falling sick. A young girl, Ania, is very ill. She lies on the floor barely moving. Her mother tries to keep her warm, gives her daughter her own rations, but disease is taking hold.

Genia looks gaunt and pale; her eyes appear sunken. She can hardly move. She too, is giving her share of food to the children. The blossoming rosiness in the cheeks of Juzia and Lucia has faded. Starved of sunlight, the buds are replaced by a pallid greyness. All three children are coughing from the continuous cold.

One more week of just bread and water passes. They have not eaten anything apart from the rations. The train stops. The doors are unbolted. Zosia drags herself towards the doors and forces herself to get off the train to find something to eat. Wojtek is with her. The two of them, supporting each other, manage to stumble a short distance.

A vast plain in the middle of nowhere stretches to the horizon, with mountains bordering the western edges. There are no houses, no village and worst of all, no people in sight. Ahead of them, in the distance, there are fields and something is growing in them, moving in the wind. They stagger towards the fields. As they get nearer, they see rows and rows of potato plants. Wojtek and Zosia fall to the ground. On their knees, and with their bare hands, they start digging up the potatoes. But the ground is cold, hard and dry which makes it difficult to dig. They use their nails to scratch the soil and with their fingers they create a hole to extract the potatoes. They clean them with their hands and on their clothes, as much as they can, and there in the field, sitting on the cold ground, they do something which would have been unthinkable back home. They bite into the unwashed, raw potatoes and eat them, delirious.

'How good they taste!' says Zosia.

'Why do we bother to cook them at home?' says Wojtek.

'Or peel them, when they taste so good like this, straight from the earth.'

They both burst into laughter. They can't stop. It is the first time they have laughed since before they left home. When they finally do stop, Wojtek says:

'Hurry, we need to get as many as we can to take back for the others.'

Zosia digs up eight more potatoes when they hear the train whistle. The beast is starting to move. The guards are shouting at them to get back on the train but they do not stop the train to wait for them. The wagon doors are left open. Zosia scoops up her harvest into her skirt and runs as fast as her legs allow. She has to get back to Genia and the children. She has to get back on the train. How could she possibly survive if she is left behind here in the middle of this vast and inhospitable wilderness? Zosia, Wojtek and the others, caught in this unexpected predicament, all start running as fast as they can. Some of them are much nearer to the train. They reach it and jump into a wagon. Wojtek pulls Zosia along to start with and then pushes her in front of him. As she is running, some of the potatoes fall to the ground hindering other runners behind. To catch the train, she will have to run much faster. The only way she can do this, is to muster all her energy and abandon the crop of potatoes in her skirt. She will need both hands to climb back into the wagon which is now speeding up. But she cannot arrive back empty handed. She has to make a split-second decision. She lets them all fall, away from anyone behind her this time, except for two potatoes she can carry, one in each hand. When she reaches the wagon, she will throw them in before climbing aboard. Relieved of the bulk of her burden and spurred on by the thought of the unacceptable alternative, she is able to run much faster. The wagon doors are open, the hands of the weak and infirm stretched out amid shouts of encouragement to the runners. Zosia is almost in reach of the hands. She throws in the two offerings she has kept. She trips slightly, and nearly falls. Recovering quickly, she makes an extra strong effort to produce a last burst of energy to run even faster, and finally, she just manages to grasp one of the hands and is pulled back onto the train.

Behind her others are still running, including Wojtek. Genia and the children are screaming. He sees them and starts to run faster. The outstretched hands of Genia and Władysław catch his, and he is hauled back into the train.

But those who do not make it are falling on the track. The sound of their horrific shrieks to stop the train pierces through the icy air. There is no chance of them making it back on the train. They are injuring themselves as they fall. Some of them cannot get up. What on earth will happen to them? Where is father? He would have been able to do something to put things right. Where is Adam? Why aren't they here to help?

Zosia catches sight of young Leszek, far from the train, running towards it. He is running fast but the train is gathering speed and moving away faster than he can run. Mrs Bienkowska is on the train. She is shouting and screaming hysterically at the guards to stop the train, to get her son. There is no hope left. The train is not going to stop. Without any hesitation, she leaps from the train. She falls on the ground, miraculously and mercifully it seems, without any serious injury. She stands up and hobbles towards Leszek who is running towards her. They reunite, hugging each other tightly.

Poor Mrs Bienkowska and poor Leszek. What else could she do? The boundless power of a mother's love. She could not leave her child behind. She would never have forgiven herself if she had. Zosia understands. She watches them as Mrs Bienkowska and Leszek become smaller and smaller dots on the snow until they disappear behind a curtain of lace snowfall.

The sight of them together, hugging each other, reminds Zosia of her father hugging her. How loved it made her feel, how safe with him. He would never have left her there alone either.

The screams of distressed family members can be heard from wagons the length of the train, but the guards do not stop it. They show no pity for those who cannot make it back, for those abandoned falling on the tracks.

There is something in Zosia's pocket. She has one small potato left. She hands it to Ania's mother. This is all she has to offer. It is pathetic giving her a raw potato for her ailing daughter, but it is all she has. Ania's mother thanks her and smiles. There is nothing Zosia can do to help them or those left behind.

Chapter 4

Zofia's Journal, March 1940

It is coal dark. I can hear the heavy breath of sleep from the huddled bodies on the floor.

Someone moves noiselessly like a smoky phantom, as we lurch from side to side.

The metal beast hisses and rumbles, jolting its cargo in and out of dreams into nightmares.

A shriek of torment pierces the night. Soulful wails for abandoned loved ones prick the air.

The imprisoned stench of urine and excrement chokes this windowless cell. My feet are wet where the pools of human waste have seeped in through my boots.

I don't know what day it is. I try to count the days and weeks I've been here.

Empty grey days merge into night. Time fades into a blurred stretch of shadow.

We are heading east. Where are they taking us? Why?

All I want is to be back home. To see Mother's eyes shining from the safe glow of the hearth, as she tells a story, Father smiling. Under their wing. I want to stroke Rex and feed the hens in the morning sunlight. But how…when, can we get back home?

It doesn't matter what day it is. It is somewhere around my sixteenth birthday. It could be today. Or maybe it was yesterday.

March – April? Time passes.

I still don't know what day it is. I no longer try to count the days and weeks.

It seems pointless.

All I want is what I don't have, what I can't have.

The most precious thing – my family, all of us together in the place that is our home.

I miss our closeness, our touch. I long for our laughter, our love.

I long for our vivid, blue-sky days together, bathed in the eternal, warm light of unbroken summer.

The sun's rays painting the scented meadows.

* * *

Zosia puts her pen and notebook back in her small bag. Half asleep, half awake, with her head pressed against a gap in the wagon wall, she feels the breeze from outside on her face. It reminds her of a time long ago when she was a child. It was June 1929.

It is a bright midsummer's morning. A fresh wind is blowing. Zosia and her father are riding together on his horse over the hills and through the fields to the market town of Storów. It is the first time she is going to Storów, a belated treat for her fifth birthday. She is sitting in front of her father on the horse, a chick enclosed in the warm nest of his arms, protected from the gusting wind. The sun has been up for hours, making the corn grow tall and turning it yellow. It stretches into the distance, where it's feathery tips brush against the sky.

She leans out from the shelter of her father's arms to look round at the sparkling river in the valley below them.

'My hat, my hat,' she cries. The cherished object is lifted and snatched from her by the wind which tosses it recklessly across the cornfield. Zosia's father stops and dismounts from the horse.

'Don't be upset, my little one. I'll get it,' he says.

He secures his trusted stallion to a nearby tree with Zosia safely on it.

'Wait here,' he says. He gives her a kiss. 'I won't be long.' He smiles. His clear eyes, as always, reassuring and full of love.

Her father strides off. She watches him wading out into the sea of corn. He is a tall man with a smiling face. His dark hair has tiny touches of silver, that look like sprinkles of glitter in the sunlight. She sits waiting on the horse, warmed by the heat of its body, feeling the rise and fall of its steady breathing. She strokes its neck.

'Papa will get the hat. Papa always puts things right.'

She chose the hat with her mother, for her fifth birthday, earlier that year. It is made of straw – a white straw boater. It is as white as the puffy clouds that are floating across the vivid sky. It has a red ribbon on it, that is tied in a bow, and flowing down the back. Zosia loves it. It is the most beautiful thing she has ever owned, and here it is being thrown about, like a tiny, multicoloured sweet onto the billowing, yellow tablecloth of the field.

She gazes at her father across the rippling landscape. The touch of the sun's strengthening rays warms her back. The wind is dropping. The silence is only broken by the whispering swish of corn, and the occasional whinny of the horse. He recovers the hat, holds it up and waves it at her. She waves back. He is striding back towards her with a beaming expression. 'Papa, my Papa, he is the best father in the world.'

They ride on to Storów. Her father is the village '*sołtys*' or mayor, and as they pass villagers on their way, they exchange a courteous greeting. He is wearing his coat of office and hat as he is attending a meeting with some important people in the afternoon. His badge of office is pinned to his lapel. It glints in the sunlight, like a beacon heralding their approach. She is proud of her father.

It is about six kilometres to Storów, where once a fortnight in the summer months, a large country market is held. He is going to look at livestock, as he needs to buy more horses for the farmstead. There are already some fifteen horses, including two old mares which, he says, will probably be unfit for much of the ploughing and harvesting work throughout the year. The stallion they are riding is his favourite and along with three other horses, only used for riding by family members. All the family ride, and Zosia has been promised a horse of her own as soon as she is old enough. 'When will that be?'

Chapter 5

They are travelling further and further north. On a few days, the sun can be glimpsed through the wooden cracks of the wagon, when it is not hidden behind stone walls of cloud. From its position in the sky, they can see that they are still heading east. This means they are travelling towards the Soviet Union, to what some of the passengers are calling 'the frozen north'.

It was cold in the wagon from the start. Now it is bitter. It must be minus ten or minus twenty. There is no fire. Snow is coming in through the cracks in the walls and icicles are forming on the inside. Juzia and Lucia are shivering. Antoni looks pitiful, his face as small and pale as the little white milk jug at home. Zosia leans against the side of the wagon and huddles up with the children. She tells them a story about somewhere hot, to transport them to the heat, at least in their minds. She tells them about Egypt, the Pharaohs and the building of the Pyramids. Genia and Wojtek have a few moments on their own. The children are enjoying the adventures of the Egyptian slaves and their mischievous cat. Lucia wriggles as she laughs at the tale, but she cannot move from the side of the wagon.

'Aunty Zosia, help! I'm stuck. My hair, it's stuck to the wall,' says Lucia.

'So is mine,' says Zosia. 'It's frozen.' Juzia and Antoni are not affected as they were not leaning on the wagon wall. Wojtek and Genia come to help. They try to release Lucia and Zosia from their ice prison but they have nothing to do it with. Using their hands, they gently rub the hair until it loosens and they are free from their trap. They rub it some more until all the ice is removed.

In the night there are screams. It has become normal. But that night is pierced by a woman's screams which do not stop. The woman's name is Jadwiga. Everyone is awake, even the children.

Genia tells Zosia that they should go and help her. Helena gives them a candle she has lit. The sisters weave their way through the bodies trying to sleep on the floor to get to Jadwiga. She looks terrified. Jadwiga's face is covered in sweat and her body is heaving. She is lying in a pool of water.

'It's coming. The baby is coming,' she cries.

The layers of thick clothing she is wearing concealed her secret, until now.

Helena has come to help. In the hours that follow, the three of them deliver a baby boy on the cold, wooden floor of the moving train. No one slept that night through the pained screams. A beautiful baby boy. They wrap him in a small towel Jadwiga has brought with her and give him to his mother. They will wash him in the morning in the boiled drinking water they get.

In the morning, Jadwiga and her son are quiet. They must be asleep, exhausted from the birth. Genia and Zosia go to see them. They are still. They look beautiful, mother and child bound together. The new-born up against his mother's breast. They are motionless. They are not breathing. Both of them are dead, frozen together from the cold. Helena makes the sign of the cross on Jadwiga and on the baby's head. She says they should give the baby a name, they call him Gabriel after the angel. The soldiers remove their bodies from the wagon and leave them in the snow by the side of the tracks.

A number of uncounted days later, the train arrives at the border with the Soviet Union, where they have to change trains. Władysław says this is because the railway gauge is different in the USSR. Just as they are about to leave the wagon, Władysław pulls out what looks like a crumpled newspaper from an inside pocket of his coat.

'Here, read this,' he says, thrusting it into Wojtek's hand. Wojtek unfolds it, taking care not to tear it. There are several pages. He looks at the them. His expression changes to one Zosia has never seen before. It is as if the light in his face has been extinguished, like the sudden, snuffed out flicker of candlelight in a room with no other light.

'You keep it,' says Władysław. Wojtek folds it up and puts it in his coat pocket.

Zosia is relieved to be released from the wretched train, if only for a short time, and breathe the icy, clean air. The cold makes the children cough more. Genia thinks they have bronchitis. There are still no passenger trains, just another cattle train. It looks even worse than the one they have left. They get on it and will have to adapt to it all over again.

As they cross the frontier between Poland and the USSR, singing of the national anthem starts in one of the wagons and spreads throughout the train.

It is becoming much colder as they head still further north. The next day the soldiers bring some wood to burn in a metal bucket. It provides heat at one end of the wagon. If only Jadwiga's baby son had been born a few days later, both of them might have survived. The passengers take it in turns to warm themselves. Zosia and the children huddle together with Helena to keep warm.

There are fewer of them in the wagon. Those left behind, the dead and the living, means the human cargo is reduced. But they do not get more rations as a result. The rations for the wagon are reduced, so that they get the same as before: one small piece of bread each per day and one cup of boiled water. Perhaps they will get more food when they arrive wherever they are taking them. They must be near their destination. Perhaps there will be hot food and fires to keep them warm.

When the train stops, Wojtek and Zosia scramble down from the wagon in the hope of finding some food. They take Juzia and Lucia with them so the girls can get some air and light. They stop at a place which seems to be very remote. There is no town, not even anything that could be called a village. There are a few small buildings in the distance. It looks like a tiny, rural hamlet in the middle of the huge, flat area that stretches out as far as the horizon for miles in all directions. Wojtek says they must be on the plains of the Russian Steppe.

There are some peasant women working in the fields. They are dressed in, shabby, drab clothes. The only spark of colour is from the bright reds, greens and blues of their patterned headscarves, which dance like jewels against the snow-bound land. It's hard to tell what age they are. Their faces, clearly once striking, with large, luminous eyes and high cheekbones, are now wind beaten and wrinkled.

They run to the peasant women and beg for food. The women look at the ragged group in front of them with sympathetic eyes. They stroke Juzia and Lucia's hair, saying melodic words in Russian '*Milen'kiye devochki*'. Zosia recognises the words, 'pretty, little girls.' She remembers some Russian from school. The women reach into their baskets and take out their own provisions for the day, offering them to Wojtek and Zosia. Homemade bread, cooked beetroot, pickled cabbage and hot soup. An unbelievable feast! They are gesturing, offering a hot, cooked meal in their homes, pointing to the houses in the distance and beckoning them to follow. Zosia and the girls are desperate to accept but Wojtek says no, there isn't time to enjoy the 'luxury' of a hot meal. The soldiers are already shouting at them from the tracks. The train is about to leave. They need to go back at once.

The women hug Juzia and Lucia and kiss them on their heads, then thrust the baskets into Zosia and Wojtek's hands. They say something in Russian, their eyes are shining with kindness and sympathy. Zosia thanks them in Polish with tear-filled eyes, full of gratitude for their generosity.

When they get back into the wagon, the girls and Zosia turn round and wave, just as the doors are closed and bolted behind them. They peer through cracks in the wagon doors and watch the women in their coloured headscarves waving until they disappear from view.

It is welcome relief. They share the food out with others, making sure the hot soup goes first to the children and the sick. Zosia helps Ania's mother prop her daughter up and feed her. Ania can only eat a few spoonfuls. She is very thin and can hardly move. Her mother tends to her day and night.

By the next day, all the food is gone. Zosia looks round the wagon. There are elderly, frail passengers and children who are sick. Disease is spreading because of the unsanitary conditions. They are dying from starvation, cold and disease.

The soldiers are now checking the wagons daily for the dead, once and sometimes twice a day. When the train stops, they remove the corpses and lay them along the side of the railway tracks in the snow, abandoned there, just as Jadwiga and her new-born Gabriel had been. Zosia remembers the funerals she had been to; celebrations of the lives of loved ones. But here there was no ceremony, no priestly blessing and no grave, only the murmur of prayers and cries of their relatives. The dead are disposed of, left to rot in the snow or be torn apart by bears and wolves. But every one of them, someone's baby, child, brother, mother, grandfather. Sometimes the train does not stop. The doors are opened and the soldiers throw the tiny bodies of dead babies and small children out of the train as it is still moving, to the sound of unimaginably, lamentable shrieks of grief. Some of the relatives jump off the train in desperation. Others sit in silence, rocking back and forth, endlessly, and staring at the walls of the wagon.

Two days after Zosia and Ania's mother fed her daughter the hot soup, Zosia wakes to find Ania's mother weeping, her arms wrapped tightly round her daughter. Ania has died in the night, cradled in her mother's embrace. When the soldiers prise Ania from her mother, drag the body off the train and dump it on the frozen ground beside the tracks, it is more than her mother can bear. She hurls herself out of the wagon and runs to her beloved child, pulling the motionless body into her arms, covering her daughter's face in kisses. It is the last Zosia sees of Ania and her mother, abandoned in the snow.

In the gloom of the wagon in the night, piercing shrieks and sorrowful cries echo, permeating the blackness of her mind. Zosia lies awake, her head full of what she has seen in the last days and weeks. The faces of Mrs Bienkowska, Leszek, Ania and her mother, Jadwiga and her baby, Gabriel pass in front of her eyes. She plunges her face into her shawl to shut out the images of wild bears ripping the flesh from those left behind.

Much later, she sleeps a little, then wakes. It is still night. She stares into the empty black space above her head. She can hear a strange sound in the distance, like the wild neighing of a horse and the clatter of galloping hooves. It is getting louder and louder. Now the hooves are banging right up against the outside of the wagon. Suddenly a huge black stallion is rearing up inside the wagon and hitting itself against the walls. It is neighing angrily, its legs flailing madly in a blind fury. It is enormous. Its body fills the wagon. Blood is pouring from open wounds in the creature's side and neck. Then she sees there is a man astride the horse. He is pulling the reins, trying to control the animal, stroking its neck, calming it, soothing it until at last, the stallion falls still. The rider is her father.

'Papa!' she screams. 'Papa! I'm here!'

She runs towards him, stretching out her arms through the murky mists of the wagon, reaching out for him.

'Papa!'

Her father turns and looks straight at her.

'Zosia, my little one,' he says in his mellow, deep voice. 'Be strong! Be brave! I love you and I am always here, looking after you. Take care of yourself and those around you. Do not despair.'

'Papa!' she screams. 'Papa!'

She wants to touch him. To hug him. To be enfolded in his arms. More than anything in the world, she wants to feel once more the warmth and security of his embrace. She reaches out her hands to touch him, but as she does so, her father and the stallion vanish and her fingers fall through empty air. In the darkness, she can still hear her father speaking to her.

'I love you, Zosia. I will be looking after you always. Never give up!'

'I love you too, Papa! I won't give up. I promise you. I am going to survive!'

But her father is gone. There is nothing there but the dark void of the ceiling.

Chapter 6

'Zosia! Wake up!'

Helena is kneeling on the floor beside her, leaning over her with a concerned expression on her face.

'Are you alright? You were shouting for your father.'

Zosia sits up. How long has she been lying on the floor? She looks over at Genia, Wojtek and the children. They are huddled together, sleeping soundly. Helena holds out her arms.

'Come here, little one. You had a bad dream. Let me stroke your head.' With her head pillowed on Helena's warm lap, Zosia gazes up at the roof of the wagon, searching the darkness for any remnant of her father, any tiny piece of him that might still be there. Gradually, the rocking of the train and Helena's gentle hands stroking her hair make her doze off again. When she next wakes, Helena is still cradling her head, protecting her from the dirty floor.

'How are you feeling?' asks Helena.

'I saw my father,' Zosia says. 'He was here, in the wagon.'

'It's alright darling. It was just a dream.'

Zosia shakes her head. 'No, it was real. He was here. I saw him. He spoke to me.'

'You love your father very much, don't you?'

Zosia nods. 'More than anything in the world.' A lump is forming in her throat. 'I miss him so much.'

'Tell me about him. What is he like? What is his name?'

Zosia takes a deep breath. It is not easy to talk about the past. It is not easy to know where to begin.

'His name was Michał, Michał Błaszczyk. He died when I was six.'

'Oh Zosia, I am so sorry!'

'He died of a broken heart, after my mother passed away. That's what everyone said. Her name was Anna. She was the love of his life.'

'What? Both your parents died when you were a child?'

'Yes. Just one year apart. My mother was ill for as long as I can remember. She had tuberculosis which forced her to spend most days in bed. She was still young, in her late thirties. She had a pale, spotless complexion and large, cornflower-blue eyes, framed by tousles of long, wavy, brown hair; the look of a slightly, dishevelled porcelain doll. She was unable to do any physical work or housework. But she used to say that she was fortunate that they had the farmstead and that they could employ a housekeeper and a cook to run the house and look after the needs of the family.

My mother's health hung over us like a shadow, but otherwise we were a very happy family. There were seven of us, including my parents. Adam was the eldest, then Genia, then my brothers Kazik and Leon, and then me. I was the baby of the family.

We lived on a '*folwark*' or farmstead on the outskirts of a village called Bortków, not far from Lwów. We lived in the main farmhouse. There were two barns, several outbuildings for the animals as well as stables for the horses, all of which was surrounded by farmland.

We all helped by doing our share of work around the house and on the farmstead, although my parents always insisted that school work had to come first. When my bothers weren't at school, they joined in with the twenty or so strong team of farmhands that father employed. Genia and I helped on the farm as much as we could. I also took care of the hens, fed them and collected the eggs. We helped in the house with the housework too. But the most important task was taking care of mother with Genia.

Despite her illness, she loved spending time with us. Some days were better than others and she was able to get up. She taught all of us to read and write before we started school. She was always interested in what we were doing and pleased to hear how we were getting on at school.

From an early age she encouraged us to read and write our own stories. We would spend days reading together and telling each other stories. She loved doing this and it was one of her main pleasures.

She read us stories by Henryk Sienkiewicz about the Teutonic knights and the Crusades, '*Krzyżacy*' from part of his trilogy, and his stories of Nero's Rome in '*Quo Vadis*.' Exciting stories about the bravery and chivalry of heroic characters.

She told us that Sienkiewicz had received the Nobel prize for Literature in 1905. Even though I didn't know what that meant exactly, I remember saying:

'He should win a prize, because I think his stories are very, very good.'

My mother smiled.

'Yes, they are, and so are your stories children. You should always carry a notebook and a pencil or pen with you, as you never know when you might want to write down what you see or your thoughts and feelings about your experiences. Perhaps one day you will write stories like Sienkiewicz, and years in the future, people will read them and love them like you love these stories.'

The winter of 1928 was very cold. The countryside was covered by a thick blanket of snow. It lasted until the beginning of March. When spring arrived, there was plenty to do on the farm, clearing the fields of rubble and stones ready for planting, repairing all the fences damaged by the snowfalls and preparing the soil for the new crops.

Adam was looking forward to the prospect of all the outdoor work. He was sixteen that year and preparing for his school exams. It meant that he would have some extra time out of school to study at home. He was going to study in the evenings so that he could help on the farmstead in the daytime. Up till then, all of us had been shielded from farm work, except during the school holidays.

My favourite time of the year was late August when the harvest was gathered in. Every pair of hands was put to best use. All the family, the farmhands and villagers worked together to bring in the wheat and store it in the barns. The hot summer seemed to last for a long time. The dry earth made it difficult to collect the sharp corn. The work day started early, soon after sunrise and lasted till late in the evening. My friends, Mila, Julcia and I were too young to do the heavy work of harvesting. The corn was gathered in and when the work was done, and the sun was still mockingly high in the sky, there would be food and drink for all and music and dance for anyone who still had any scrap of energy left. Throughout the day my friends and I came around with welcomed trays of, refreshing drinks and baskets of freshly baked bread and cake for the harvesters, which we had made with Maria, Mila's mother. Everyone had a part to play and ours was a very important one as the workers needed to have refreshment and rest.

A young housemaid also lived with us at the farmstead. Her name was Kasia and she came to us when she was sixteen. She helped the Cook in the kitchen and did housework and laundry, as well as tending to Anna.

The same year Kasia came to live with us, Piotr came to live with us too. He was apprenticed to Franek, our general handyman, who had been with our family for years. Piotr must have been about seventeen when he joined our household. He helped Franek around the farmstead and could turn his hand to almost any task. According to my sister, there was an instant chemistry between Kasia and Piotr, but I was too young to notice this of course. Genia must have been right, because a year later they announced their intention to marry. My parents thought it was an excellent idea. They said that Kasia and Piotr were clearly very much in love and well suited. My parents suggested that they could use the farmhouse and grounds for their wedding celebrations and that they would provide the wedding banquet for them.

There was great excitement as plans were made. The parents and siblings of Kasia and Piotr's families were all invited as guests of honour and to take part in the planning. There hadn't been a wedding at the farmstead before. Kasia's sisters, Genia, Mila and Julcia and I were all going to be bridesmaids. My friends and I were thrilled. None of us had ever been bridesmaids.

My father was talking about borrowing tables and chairs from friends and neighbours and from the church hall. I remember him and Piotr making a pair of trestles, then cutting and sanding a long piece of wood to create a long table. My brothers helped father and Piotr to set up the tables for the reception behind the main house, overlooking the small lake.

On the day, everything looked beautiful, the tables were decorated with pretty cloths and the wild flowers we had picked. Coloured lanterns, clusters of small, pink flowers and white lilies from the garden were hanging from the trees. It looked like a fairy-tale scene. Its shimmering reflection was mirrored in the lake.

The bride and groom went to the village church in a horse and cart bedecked with even more flowers and garlands. Kasia looked like a princess, dressed in a beautiful, white dress that she and Genia had made together. She wore a little crown of tiny white flowers and rosebuds in her hair and carried a delicate bouquet of the same flowers. Piotr looked very smart in his dark suit, white shirt and tie, as he accompanied his bride in their carriage.

We followed in another carriage. Even the horses had bows tied in their manes. The sun was shining brightly. The only shade came from the trees lining the road towards the church. The village church was full, family members and friends were packed into the pews. The service, was conducted by the parish priest, Father Paul. The couple made their vows. I remember seeing my parents smiling at one another. Perhaps they were thinking about their own wedding. When Kasia and Piotr came out of the church, we all threw handfuls of rose petals at them and there were roses strewn all along the path leading from the church to their carriage.

Music played through the night. A band of musicians performed all kinds of music: joyful music for the bride and groom's first dance, folk music and songs that all the guests joined in with. Joy and laughter filled the whole farmstead and all the villagers came from miles around to join in the celebrations.

Mila, Julcia and I thought it was the best day of our lives. We were wearing flowing peach-coloured dresses, trimmed with lace and taffeta, that my mother had bought from the haberdasher's and made with the help of Genia and Kasia. Our heads were crowned with daisies and tiny rosebuds. We ran about and danced and sang in the sunny, unending day. I saw Adam dancing with our neighbour's daughter, Katarina. I noticed the two of them staring into each other's eyes, but I was far too absorbed, and far too young to understand.'

Chapter 7

'The following year, in the winter of 1929, everything changed. Not long before Christmas, my mother's health got worse. She stayed in bed for several weeks, unable to come downstairs. Genia, Kasia and I looked after her. We all took turns, sitting with her in the dark evenings. My father never left her side. We listened to her reading by lamplight, if she was able to, or recounting stories from memory and from her imagination. She got tired and had to lie quietly to rest and get her breath back. Then one of us would take over the reading, choosing one of mother's favourite passages, some of which we also knew by heart.

The doctor visited frequently. He prescribed more medicines and was encouraging. But I later learned that they were only to relieve her pain. There was no cure. My father told us that there was nothing more the doctor could do. God would look after her. We prayed that God would make her well. She lingered in this state for five days, getting weaker each day.

Breathing became difficult. Every breath seemed like a huge effort. Her chest heaved up and down. We stayed with her through the night, watching and praying, till we fell asleep on the floor beside her bed.

Genia's scream woke me. I looked up. Genia was standing at the end of the bed trembling. Father was kneeling at the side, crying. I moved towards mother. There was a trace of a smile on her beautiful face but her stony eyes did not shine.

No sound came out of my mouth. Father kissed her and gazed at her for a long time. Genia followed. Then the others. My turn came. I touched her hands which had been placed across her chest. It reminded me of pictures I had seen of angels. Her hands were cold and hard. I kissed her face. It was wet and salty from all the tears that had fallen on it.

I was five when she died. I could not understand what I had seen. I couldn't understand that she was gone and was never coming back. She was thirty-nine.

'Her passing was peaceful,' said Adam, hugging me tightly.

My father had lost his truelove. He stayed in the house for days, sitting in the chair near the hearth, staring at the flickering flames. He barely spoke. I watched him.

'Come my darling, come and sit on my lap.'

I climbed up and snuggled in his warmth.

One afternoon, a few months later, I was sent down to the orchard at the far side of the lake to pick apples for a pie Kasia was making for dinner.

'Eight apples, choose the ripest don't forget, one for each of us.' Genia's words stuck in my head: 'Eight apples', not the usual 'nine' and 'one for each of us.' There were now only eight of us with Kasia and Piotr.

As I walked down towards the lake, I saw father sitting on the bench at the water's edge. He was staring out across the water and when he heard me coming, he looked round slightly startled. I saw there were tears rolling down his face.

He put his arms round me, and lifted me up onto the bench beside him. We sat there in silence for a long while, watching the lake and the light fading above the treetops.

There was a little sparrow, I remember. It landed on the water close to us, fluttering its wings and sending up a fountain of sparkling droplets. It cocked its head at us, as if to say hello, and then it flew away.

One day towards the end of the autumn of 1930, father came in from working on fixing the barn. Adam was still out. He had gone to the Ironmonger's for some new hinges for the barn doors. Kazik and Leon were not back from school. Genia and I were in the living room. Genia was sewing and I was doing my homework. Father came in. He got himself a cup of water and sat down in his chair. Moments later, he started groaning and clutching his chest. He fell to the floor, writhing and shouting in agony. He asked Genia to give him some '*spirytus*' to rub on his chest to ease the pain. Frantically, we searched through all the cupboards in the kitchen but could not find any.

'Zosia, go to the grocer and get some *spirytus*, quickly, run!' screamed Genia. I did run. I ran as fast as I could, without thinking about anything except saving my father. When I reached the shop, it was shut. I banged on the door and shouted,

'Help, help, Mr. Wisniewski, my father is ill. He needs spirytus for his chest!'

Mr. Wisniewski got the spirytus and drove me back at great speed in his own horse and carriage. Genia met us at the door in tears.

'It's too late,' she said.

Father lay motionless on the floor. His face pale as the milky moon. I fell on my father's body, hugging it and crying. I will never forget the expression on his face, so calm, so still, so at peace. My beloved Papa, so cold on the floor.

It was as if my world had ended. I was six years old. Why had this happened? Why did God do this? What had I, or any of us done to deserve losing both our beloved parents? First the shock of mother's death, and now, less than a year later, father.

I would frequently go and sit on the bench by the lake, taking comfort from being there. I would often look for the sparrow we had seen but I could only see it in my mind's eye. I drew a picture of the sparrow flapping its wings and creating a fountain. I drew another of my mother and father walking hand in hand by the lake, smiling.

Adam became my saviour. He was the eldest member of what remained of the family. But he was not old enough to be in charge of it, legally. We were a family of five orphans. A solicitor from Lwów was in charge of us and there had to be a guardian living with us, until Adam reached the age of eighteen. He would then have to sign papers and would officially take on the role as head of the family. His eighteenth birthday was only several months away, which meant the guardian did not have to stay very long.

All our lives changed completely. Adam had to take on responsibility for the family and take over my father's role in every respect as head of the household. All of us had to become more responsible for the running of the farmstead. Genia looked after the house. I helped all I could. Kazik and Leon said I should do the cooking, but Adam stood up for me, calling them immature and saying that it would be totally inappropriate for a girl of six who had barely started school to take on such duties. Fortunately, Kasia and Piotr continued living with us. Adam had to manage the workforce and supervise the running of the farmstead. For the following eight years, from 1931 to 1939, we all worked hard together to keep the farmstead successful as our parents would have wanted.

In the early summer of the year following father's death, Genia, at the age of sixteen, married Wojtek. There were modest wedding festivities out of respect for the still recent deaths of our parents. After they were married, Wojtek came to live at the farmstead and they soon started a family of their own.'

Chapter 8

Eight weeks and over 1,500 miles after they had left Bortków, the train stops. The sign on the narrow station platform is in Russian and reads 'Noszul.' None of them have ever heard of a place called Noszul.

It must be early April. Back home in Poland, the meadows would have been bursting with wild flowers: forget-me-nots, daisies, cornflowers. The trees would be heavy with clusters of pink and white blossoms. The fields would be filled with gambolling lambs.

In Noszul, there are no signs of spring. In Noszul it is still winter, the land still locked in snow and ice. It is bitterly cold. Colder than anything or anywhere Zosia has ever experienced. Wojtek says they must be very far north, in the subpolar region, near the Arctic Circle. He thinks they are somewhere in the depths of Siberia.

They are ordered off the train and told to take all their belongings with them. Zosia has none, only the clothes she is wearing and her small bag.

The train wagon doors are unbolted and slid open. The sight that greets her eyes is astonishing. After the long weeks incarcerated in the dark wagons, the intense brightness of the snowbound trees and surrounding mountains is even more of a shock to the senses. The sky is white. The air is crystal, clean and pure. She breathes it in deeply, slowly, appreciatively, gorging on its freshness. The overpowering, pine scent cuts through the icy air, filling it with its refreshing smell. Her eyes begin to adapt to the light, she stares at the unexpected sight in front of her. Thousands and thousands of fir trees covered in snow, stretching out into the distance, as far as the eye can see.

'Welcome to the endless Virgin Forests of Siberia,' says a grinning soldier.

On the partly, snow-cleared platform, Zosia sees small remnants of the bundles of clothes and personal items people have managed to preserve. But more conspicuous, and far more pitiful to her, are the people, or rather, what they have become over the course of the two-month journey. What is left of them? The starved, unwashed, impoverished shapes of displaced men, women and children, the remains of the eroded human cargo. Some of them are hobbling, barely able to walk.

The soldiers herd them off the platform towards a line of open army trucks. Zosia follows Genia, the children and Wojtek, who are climbing on at the back of a truck.

As they are being herded towards the waiting truck, Zosia realises that Helena is not with them. She turns to look for her and sees Helena, a little way behind them, being jostled out of the way by the press of people. She looks small and old and frightened.

'Keep up, Babcia Helena!' Zosia shouts to her. 'Don't get separated!'

Helena starts pushing through the crowds of people, but before she has time to catch up with Zosia and her family, the soldiers bar her way. Helena cries out in alarm, but the soldiers are pushing her away from Zosia towards a different truck.

'Don't worry,' Zosia shouts. 'I'll come and find you.'

Genia and the children are already on the truck. The children are shivering. Zosia has no choice but to climb in after them. She turns to wave goodbye to her friend, tears stinging her eyes. Helena is smiling and crying and waving at them.

'Goodbye, my darlings,' she calls over the heads of the crowd.

'Goodbye, Babcia Helena,' the children call back to her. 'Goodbye!'

'We'll find you!' calls Zosia. 'I promise! We'll come and find you.'

Part 3

Before and After II

Chapter 1

There must be about forty people crammed in the back of the open truck. It is bitterly cold. Genia and Wojtek wrap the children inside their coats to keep them warm. Only Lucia's head is visible. She is peeping out from her father's coat. Antoni, safe with his mother. Zosia enfolds Juzia in her coat and huddles together with the family.

The people from the train are being packed on to the trucks. When all the trucks are full, the convoy sets off on a narrow road that leads into the forest. The road has been cleared. There are shoulder-deep mounds of snow piled on either side. Stretching out in all directions are thick forests of towering, snow-loaded firs. The white sky at the station earlier in the morning is now filling up with threatening, heavy clouds. Minutes later, snow starts coming down fast. A tarpaulin in the truck serves as some protection.

After several hours in the convoy, the road comes to an end and they are transferred onto sleighs, pulled by tractors. The sleighs are pulled through deep snow for miles, further and further into the forest.

The invisible sun sets. It is the time between day and night, when all turns from white to grey, when it is easy to lose orientation. Dusk is falling. Everything looks at its worst. The sky is bloated with suffocating clouds that hang like a leaden net enclosing them in these gloomy surroundings. A frozen river contains a narrow trickle of mercury-like, silver water.

After another hour or so, the tractors come to a halt somewhere deep in the dense forest. Armed soldiers stand guard in front of a high metal gate. Bars run from top to bottom. There is barbed wire along the upper edge. The soldiers count them through the gate.

In a clearing ahead of them there are rows of small buildings. What passes for accommodation in this inhospitable place, are dark and dilapidated barracks.

Zosia and her family are allocated one room for the six of them, no more than eight-foot square. The walls are made of wooden logs. The gaps between the logs are packed with moss. Where there is no moss, the wind whistles through and the snow is coming in. The floor is bare earth. There are no windows. In one corner, there is a table and two small chairs. Set against the wall, there is a wooden bed. There is no mattress. There is no fire and the room offers little escape from the cold. It smells damp and musty.

Antony is shivering and crying.

'Mama, I'm hungry,' he says. Genia looks at Wojtek.

'I don't like it here, I'm cold,' says Lucia.

'When can we go back home?' says Juzia.

Genia's eyes glisten. She turns away and wipes her face quickly.

'I don't know. Soon, I hope.' she says.

Zosia and Wojtek go out to look for Helena.

'What is this place? Where are we?' she says.

'It's a Camp, a Labour Camp…somewhere…at the end of the world,' he says.

Helena is nowhere to be seen. Neither are any of the others who were in the same wagon.

'We'll look again tomorrow,' says Wojtek.

'Every day, until we find her. She must be frightened on her own.'

'We'll find her. She's probably asleep in one of the barracks by now.'

It becomes dark. The temperature drops. They huddle up on the bed to keep warm, and try to sleep. The one blanket between them on the bed is harsh and gritty. Theirs from home, used to clean the floor in the train, lies, long ago abandoned somewhere along the side of the tracks. The children fall sleep. Zosia lies awake, she gets a little sleep. In the night, she wakes. Questions are filling her head.

Where were they? Why? What was going to happen to them? How long were they going to be there? How could they ever get back home?

She had no answers except to one question: 'Where on earth were they?'

Never before had the familiar saying been more appropriate than now, 'Where the devil says good night.'

Chapter 2

The following morning, a shrill whistle and shouting outside wakes them.

'Rations, get your rations.' Zosia looks at her watch. It is six o'clock.

'I'll go,' says Wojtek. He picks up his identity card and the scrap of paper they were given when they arrived with the scribbled ration allowance for the family.

'I'll go with you,' says Zosia.

Outside the barrack, in the murky darkness and icy temperatures, a queue of blanketed, shivering shapes is forming beside a table and some wooden crates, where an urn is discharging clouds of steam. A brown sack on one of the crates must be the food. There are two soldiers, one behind the table and one next to the crate. They are handing out the rations.

Zosia and Wojtek join the queue. Zosia looks around for Helena. She does not see her.

Wojtek hands the grim-faced Russian soldier the ration paper. The soldier reaches into the sack, pulls out some bread, weighs it and hands it to Wojtek without a word.

'Can I get the rations for all my family? There are six of us.'

'Ha!' the soldier says. 'That is the ration for the family.'

Wojtek looks at it and walks away.

Zosia picks up a jug, fills it with the hot contents from the urn and takes two cups.

Back at the barrack, Genia looks in disbelief at the small loaf of rye bread and the jug of hot water. She turns to her husband.

'Is that all?' Wojtek says nothing and looks away. An odd silence follows. Without a word, Genia divides the loaf into six portions and gives it out, the bigger portions for the children. Juzia and Lucia gobble it up and are looking round for more. Antoni is asking for more.

'This is all we have,' says Genia.

'We have to be content with what we have been given,' says Wojtek.

Zosia pours the tepid, boiled water into the cups and gives one to the children and one to her sister and brother-in-law.

She overhears Genia whispering to Wojtek.

'We have to make sure the children get enough to eat. They can have my lunch ration.'

'Mine too,' says Wojtek.

'And mine,' says Zosia.

When no more food is handed out at lunch time or in the evening, they realise with horror that the ration handed out in the morning was supposed to be for the whole day. There is no more food until the next morning.

In the evening, all that comes is more tepid water to drink but nothing to eat. Antoni is asking for milk. Zosia huddles up with her nieces on the bed. When they fall asleep, she feels their soft breathing and hears their stomachs rumbling.

Genia is cradling Antoni, he is asleep.

'What are we going to do?' Genia is saying to Wojtek. 'We have to think of something. We can't let the children starve.' Wojtek puts his arms around his wife and child and hugs them.

After a while, he says, 'Tomorrow, I'll look. There must be some potatoes or beetroot in the fields. We can boil them and make soup. And the children can have my share of the bread from now on. I can manage without.'

'No! You've got to eat too! We need to get more food from somewhere. We can't do that if you're starving yourself to death.'

'Don't worry. I'll get more food tomorrow,' he says.

Genia doesn't say anything.

Later when Wojtek is asleep, Genia says to Zosia:

'What's he saying? There are no fields with potatoes or anything. There's nothing here except trees. And everything is covered in metres of snow...What are we going to do? We can't let the children starve.'

The next morning, Genia tells Zosia her idea and what Wojtek and her have decided to do.

'We are going to reduce our share of the bread, we'll have half of our portion in the morning, and save the extra portions for the children to have in the evening.'

'And my half portion too,' says Zosia.

They collect the morning rations and are putting aside the three half portions for the children for the evening.

'Mama,' says Juzia. 'Can I have that if you don't want it, please?'

'Mama, can I have some?' says Lucia.

'We are saving it for you, for later. We're not going to get anything else to eat today. You can look forward to having it tonight.'

'I'm hungry now,' says Antoni.

Being only two, he has no notion of 'later'. Juzia and Lucia agree with him, although Juzia is old enough to know better, and at least, to understand what her parents are trying to do.

'They're starving,' says Wojtek. 'Who can blame them?'

Genia sticks to her plan.

'No, it's for later. You'll be pleased to have it tonight. You will thank me.'

Before they leave the room, Genia tells Zosia that she is not going to take any risks with the precious rations. She wraps the portions of remaining bread in a piece of crumpled, brown paper she found on the floor and hangs it from an old, rusty nail that is sticking out of the uneven, wooden ceiling to keep it safe from thieving hands. If she puts it high enough, she reasons, the children won't be able to reach it. If anyone gets in during the day and steals the bread, it will be a disaster as none of them will have anything to eat in the evening. Zosia reassures her that no one knows the food is there. Why would anyone come into their room? Genia is uncertain if her plan will work, but she is pleased that only her, Wojtek and Zosia can reach it if they stand on a chair. 'This will work, it has to work,' she says.

In the evening, after a full, hard day's work, they come back to find that the bread is there, undetected and untouched. They give it to the children.

Despite Genia's plan, the children are not well. Lucia has become very thin. She is being sick. Juzia is even sicker. Her face is drained of any colour. Both of them have welts on their arms and legs due to not having any proper food and vitamins. Juzia is complaining of stomach pains and has chronic diarrhoea. Genia asks for her daughter to be seen by a doctor in the medical centre. She cannot go with Juzia herself, even if she had been allowed to, as missing work would mean she would not reach her quota and therefore not get any rations. Genia sends Juzia to the medical centre on her own.

On the first day at the Camp, at 6.30am, they all have to be at the meeting point, a small clearing a ten-minute walk along a narrow path from the barracks. The soldiers divide them into groups of ten. The children are put together in a separate group. In Zosia's group there are young and old women, old men, and teenagers. A soldier gives them each a handsaw and instructs them to cut all the branches off from a felled trunk. No one asks how to use the saw. Most of them have probably never used one before. The tree looks like it has been lying there a long time, submerged in snow, and as they begin removing the snow, its withered branches are revealed. Zosia starts to saw a small branch. The teeth of the saw get stuck and caught on the bark. But as she pulls the saw towards her, it cuts a groove in the wood. She pushes the saw in the groove and eventually manages to create a smoother movement, deepening the groove, until finally, the branch falls off. She cuts another and another. Each time she gets better and faster. She cuts thicker branches. The soldier tells the group that they have to cut all the branches from two large trunks. It takes them all day.

Within a couple of days, using the handsaw has become easier. But on the third day, the instructions change. Each group now has to cut branches from six trunks and they have to collect and stack the branches into piles. They will have to work much faster and for much longer. A few hours into the morning, Zosia has blisters on her hands. It is a miracle that they manage to achieve the target set.

At the end of the long day, in the fading light, Zosia is returning to the barracks. It is quiet round the barracks. She cannot hear any voices from their room. She must be the first one back.

She opens the door. An unexpected sight: in the middle of the room, one of the chairs is stood on top of the table. The bundle of bread is gone. Wojtek's book and what looks like their ration papers are lying on top of the chair.

Who did this? Who could've come in and stolen the bread?

Whoever it was, it was someone who needed to use the chair and book to reach the ceiling.

The gritty blanket on the bed moves. Juzia's head and arms come out from under it. Until that moment, she had been completely covered. She is still asleep.

Did Juzia steal the bread? Surely not? It would have been too difficult for her to lift the chair onto the table by herself. She was ill, she wouldn't have had enough strength to climb up on to the chair. But if she had, the food must have still been out of reach. She would have had to climb down and find something to give her a few more inches of extra height – the book and the ration booklet. Even then, Juzia would probably still not have been able to reach it, unless …she must have stood on tiptoe and stretched to her limit. Genia is going to be furious.

Juzia stirs.

'Juzia, what happened?'

'It was me Aunty Zosia, I took the bread. I'm scared. Mother will be angry.

Zosia sits on the bed next to her niece, puts her arms around her and hugs her.

'I've done a terrible thing…I was so hungry.'

'It's alright. Your mother will forgive you.'

'No, she won't…'

'Your mother loves you.'

'Lucia and Antoni have nothing to eat tonight. I'm so sorry.'

'She'll forgive you, you were unwell,' says Zosia. 'Did you go to the Medical Centre?'

'Yes,' says Juzia. 'But it was closed when I got there, so I came here and…I feel so guilty. I saw the bundle up there. I imagined biting into the bread, tasting it, swallowing it. I thought it would make me feel better. I knew it was wrong but I couldn't stop myself. I'm so sorry.'

Zosia strokes her niece's head.

'Don't be afraid, she will understand.'

But when Genia sees that the saved bundle of bread is gone, she is beside herself with anger and disbelief.

'Who would've done this?' she shouts. 'What are we going to do? What are the children going to eat?'

Zosia glances over at Juzia, who is sitting on the edge of the bed, staring down at the floor in silence. Finally, in a small, frightened voice, Juzia says:

'It was me, Mama.'

'Juzia?' Her mother stares at her. 'Juzia! How *could* you! How could you steal from your own brother and sister?'

Juzia starts to cry. 'I'm so sorry. I was so hungry, Mama. I felt so sick.'

Genia sits down on one of the chairs and puts her head in her hands. The others are all still and silent.

What seems like a very long few minutes later, Genia gets up and moves towards Juzia. She looks at her daughter's stricken face, and her anger slowly melts away. She puts her arms around her and hugs her tightly.

'I'm so sorry, my darling. I'm so sorry.'

Chapter 3

The Russian work ethic is, '*U nas kto ne rabotaet tot i ne kushaet.*' 'No work, no food.' A clear message. The work is set by the Camp and the quotas are high. Those who don't fulfil their quota, don't get any rations. The regime in the Labour Camp is strict. There are no exceptions, young or old, sick or not. Everyone works a long, demanding day to earn their rations, pathetic as they are.

Juzia and Lucia have to collect the twigs and small branches which break off the trees as they are felled. In the evening, these are used for burning outside the barracks to keep warm. The girls stack them into piles, put them into crates and carry them to the barracks. Each of them has to fill five wooden crates every day to fulfil their quota. It takes them all day.

To begin with, Genia collects moss for the barrack insulation and stocks the wood piles for the evening fires. After one day, she is sent, along with some of the other women, to make bricks. This is not easy when the soil is frozen and overlaid with several metres of snow. The women have to dig down through the snow to reach the soil, then mix it with water to create mud. They add pine needles to help form the mixture into bricks. Sometimes children are sent to collect the pine needles and mix the soil with water. It takes several days for the bricks to dry, then they have to be carried in sacks up a ladder to the top of the building that is being constructed. It is dirty and dangerous work.

Everyone else over the age of sixteen works in the forest, including Wojtek and Zosia. They have to fell the trees and transport them to the saw mills. The forests are thick with tall, fir trees. Although it must be early May, temperatures are well below freezing, -20 degrees Celsius. There are no machines, everything is done by hand. The whole exercise seems to be painstakingly inefficient, much like the whole experience of being there is turning out to be.

First, the trees are sawn by hand. This is done by men and women. All the time, the unpredictable threat of falling trees hangs over them. Once the trees are down, Zosia and other young girls cut off all the small to medium-sized branches from the felled trunks with handsaws. On a large tree, it takes several hours for a group of six to remove all the branches and stack them into piles. Then the trunks have to be rolled to an area near the river to be transported to the mill. The land is slightly slopped towards the river, but in places it is flat or uphill. The river is frozen and Zosia and the other girls have to slide the logs along the ice. She has to run on the ice, pushing and controlling the movement of the logs along the ice to the distant mills. There is no danger of falling in the icy water. The ice is metres thick.

The lack of food is a constant torment. No fruit, no vegetables, no meat, no fish, no dairy, the list is as endless as the forest itself. Nothing could be so different from the abundance taken for granted back home. The only variation to the meagre diet is the occasional drink of weak, watery tea with a sugar lump. The daily ration is 800 grams of bread, per person. After a few weeks, they all have clusters of welts on their arms, legs, around their knees and on the trunks of their bodies as a result of vitamin deficiency.

Seeing the children's smooth bodies disfigured by welts and blisters and seeing them starving before her eyes, is becoming more and more difficult for Genia to bear. One early evening, she says:

'Zosia, let's go and see if we can find something to eat for the children? Perhaps, we'll find some berries or mushrooms.'

'Maybe,' says Zosia.

'Children, you stay in the barrack, don't go out. Your father will be back soon. Tell him we've gone to look for food. We won't be long.'

Past the rows of barracks, where the lines of unfelled trees begin, the thick tangle of the forest starts. Around the base of a knotted group of tall fir trees, the snow is hard to dig away with their hands but that is where mushrooms grow. There are none here, just the bald, frozen earth with nothing more to offer. Nearby, on an old fallen trunk, a group of white-spotted, red toadstools flourish. They are poisonous but it means there could be edible mushrooms nearby. They do not find any. Fallen pine cones litter the snow like the fallen leaves of autumn. They collect the cones. The pine nuts can be eaten. Uncertain about the safety of eating some of the berries they see, they pick them anyway from the branches of trees. They will check later whether they are safe or not. They are pleased with the little harvest they have gathered. It will provide some protein and some vitamins. At least they are not coming back empty-handed.

The sun, rarely visible through the obstinate layers of thick cloud, sets. It is dusk.

'We should go back,' says Genia. 'It's getting dark, I can hardly see.'

'Me too. It must be the fog,' says Zosia.

'I can't remember the way back. I can't even see a short distance in front of us,' says Genia.

'Where are you Genia? I can't see you.'

'I can't see you,' says Genia. Zosia walks towards her sister's voice and grasps her hands in the semi-darkness.

'Which way is it?' says Genia.

'I don't know. I can't see anything,' says Zosia.

'The fog is so thick. I can't see either.'

'It might be this way?' Zosia points to her left.

'It can't be far. We didn't go far. Let's try calling out. Someone at the camp might hear us.'

They start walking in what they think is the direction of the camp. They call out for help, stumbling over the gnarled roots of the trees. Zosia's fear grows. The thought of being lost, meandering forever in the forest and perhaps wandering off in the wrong direction, miles from the camp, terrifies her. They could be eaten by wolves or bears if they don't freeze to death first. Striving to get back feels endless.

Eventually they hear Wojtek calling:

'Genia, Genia! Zosia, Zosia! where are you?'

'Wojtek, here we are, over here!' shouts Genia.

Wojtek moves towards their cries. After a couple of minutes, he reaches them.

'Thank God you are safe,' he hugs them.

'Wojtek, I can't see,' says Genia.

'We can't see in this thick fog. We couldn't find our way back,' says Zosia.

He holds onto them firmly.

'It's alright, I'm here now. Just hold on to me. It's not far.' He guides them carefully back through the forest.

They move forward clinging on to Wojtek. A while later, they hear the children's voices calling out to them. A few steps further and they can smell the fire and then they feel its heat. Juzia and Lucia are touching them, hugging them.

'I still can't see,' says Zosia.

'I can't see you, children,' says Genia.

When they are inside the barrack, Wojtek says:

'Don't be afraid. It's temporary, only a temporary loss of vision. You will be able to see normally soon. It's night blindness, caused by the lack of vitamins.'

Genia and Zosia are pleased to learn that the children eat the pine nuts. There is enough for all of them. Genia says that they will check if the berries are safe tomorrow.

That night Zosia closes her eyes and tries to sleep. Will Genia and her be able to see in the morning? She will have to wait till then to know if Wojtek is right.

Most days Zosia works with an old Russian man called Juzef. He looks very old to her. Much, much older than her father. His face is heavily lined, like a freshly ploughed field, and when he laughs, the lines crumple into even deeper ravines. He is not like the soldiers who do not seem to care about the deportees. Juzef says he likes nearly everyone he meets, no matter who they are or where they come from. He respects them until they do something to lose his trust. He says he is a born optimist.

Zosia works with him most days and he calls her, '*vnuchka*', which she guesses means, granddaughter, as it sounds like almost the same word in Polish.

Juzef drives the carts that take the workers to and from different parts of the forest for work. When the deportees complain about the cold, he often jokes with them:

'What's the matter? You don't like our winter? Don't worry it'll soon be summer. Winter lasts ten months and then all the rest is summer, summer, glorious summer!'

All the work they do is counted, measured and recorded for the quotas. So many bricks to make, so many trees to fell, so many trees to remove the branches from and transport, so many sacks of sawn-off branches. The forest obliges and provides an infinite and inexhaustible source of work for them.

Some of the felled trunks are cut into shorter logs. These have to be piled onto carts which are pulled by horses and taken to other storage sites. In the freezing cold, when the rivers are frozen solid, one of Zosia's jobs is to run behind a cart loaded with logs. She has a lantern and her job is to signal to the driver, by waving the lantern, if any of the logs fall off the cart.

One day Zosia is running behind the cart on the icy ground. It is hard and slippery. The snow is seeping into her boots. She has little grip on the ice and her feet are unfeeling from the cold. She is running behind the cart with the lantern when some of the logs fall off the cart, tripping her up as they roll on the ground in front of her. She falls over. One of the logs lands on her leg with a loud crack. Her scream of agony shatters the silence and sets off a flock of wild geese.

Juzef stops the cart immediately and rushes to her aid. After gently examining her leg, he confirms what she already feared – that the bone is broken. They are hundreds of miles from any town or hospital and there is no chance of getting any proper medical help but Juzef acts quickly. He snaps two branches from a nearby tree, places them on either side of Zosia's broken leg and secures them in place with his scarf. He then carefully lifts her onto the cart. An owl shrieks as he drives back to the camp as quickly as he can.

The 'Medical Centre' consists of a corner in one of the barracks. The staff look young and inexperienced. The 'nurse' seems barely trained and the 'paramedic' seems even less experienced. They examine her leg. After a short consultation, the paramedic announces that her leg is badly fractured in a number of places and that it will need to be amputated below the knee. A fierce argument ensues between Juzef and the medics. Zosia doesn't know what Juzef is saying exactly, but it is clear he is refusing to back down. The paramedic eventually shrugs his shoulders in exasperation and turns away. Free to go, Juzef lifts Zosia and carries her back outside to the cart.

As the old man is lifting her onto the cart, they are joined by a young man. He looks at Zosia.

'What's going on father? I heard shouting.'

Juzef tells his son what has happened.

'I'm not leaving her with those butchers,' he says to his son. 'I'll take care of her myself.'

Back at the barracks, he makes a new splint. He strips the bark from the pieces of wood and saws them down to a better size, then binds up the leg once more so that the broken bone is held firmly in position. The next day he returns with a pair of crutches he has made for her.

Very gradually, Zosia's leg begins to heal. It isn't perfect. The bone has grown together a little awkwardly. After about a month, she can walk without the crutches. She has a slight limp and her left ankle is still swollen compared to her other one, but she is deeply grateful to Juzef that she still has her leg in one piece.

Chapter 4

Weeks, months of murky days in the Labour Camp nail them into a world of permanent twilight, a purgatory, somewhere between life and death.

One morning, there is an unexpected sight, one Zosia has only seen a few times since leaving home. It is the cloudless, clear expanse above her head. The surprise of a rare blue-sky day appears out of nowhere. The tree tops are visible. The shroud of misty cloud removed like the veil from a bride's face to reveal true beauty. It is more than welcome and succeeds in lifting her spirits a little.

Juzia and Lucia are outside chasing each other around the previous night's extinguished fire. Lucia lets out a squeal as Juzia catches her. Their tinkling giggles remind her of them playing on the farmstead. Lucia takes up the chase to catch her big sister. The sun shines on their once golden hair. The sun and sky conspire to remind her of what could have been. Almost like being home. She cannot forget that place filled with blue skies, where the sun shines for long days on end.

They must be getting nearer to the 'glorious' Siberian summer. Zosia longs for the heat of the unending, summer days back home, among the flowering meadows and the fields full of crops, where the sun warms her body as she plays by the banks of the stream and the lake. For where they all sweat in the heat of the midday sun as they help with the bounteous harvest of golden corn, where they seek out shade to offer respite from the relentless sun. For where, in the early mornings, she finally gallops her long-awaited, dappled horse across the lush, grassy hills.

Many of the deportees are showing signs of exhaustion. Sickness and disease are spreading. Many are too ill to carry on working. Many are dying.

As those able to work trudge up the hill after an exceptionally long morning cutting down trees, a strange smell reaches their nostrils. It is a nondescript smell, but remotely recognisable, vaguely resembling that of soggy cabbage; a vegetable which is supposed to be very common in this part of the world. Despite this, they have not had any since they arrived.

They move nearer, steam is rising from the large metal urn.

'Food, food and what's more, hot food,' Zosia feels excited as her stomach rumbles in anticipation. They are ordered to line up. As they wait, they try to identify the elusive smell.

'It's not pheasant. What I wouldn't give for a piece of roasted pheasant,' says a deportee.

'It can't be pheasant. They're intelligent creatures, there aren't any here,' says another.

'It's far too cold for pheasants anyway.'

'It'll be soup, but it's not mushroom soup,'

'No, that smells good,' another deportee joins in.

The talk of pheasants reminds her of the time she went with her father to the market town of Storów. The stalls were full of all kinds of unfamiliar smells, including pheasants. This didn't smell like pheasant.

'It'll be chicken soup, if we're lucky,' the first deportee says.

The nearest they can come up with and the only one that they can agree on is that it must be cabbage. The faint smell of cabbage stirs memories of a meal they have back home: '*Gołąbki*,' cabbage leaves stuffed with minced meat and rice in a rich tomato and mushroom sauce. They joke down the ranks.

'The Bolsheviks are cooking us *gołąbki*!' The thought of any cooked, hot food overwhelms them.

'Stand in line,' shouts the guard. The metal urn, glints in the sunlight, like a silver trophy. The ladle catches the sun's rays as the guard spoons out the precious rations. It reminds her of something long ago, sparkling in the sunlight. It was something in Storów? She can't quite remember. It will come back.

Zosia's turn eventually comes. She holds out the small bowl and watches as half a ladle of the colourless liquid is poured in. When she tastes it, it tastes of nothing, but has a hint of cabbage flavour to it. Is it just the usual boiled water? The cabbage flavour might be due to the remains of old cabbage leaves cooked in the urn some time ago? It is not what any of them imagined, and far beyond disappointment. In spite of this, the hot watery, so-called 'soup' provides welcome relief from the incessant hunger and cold. With the small piece of daily bread, from their evening ration and a sugar cube that they are given, it offers some respite. It is better than nothing and they are grateful for what they have received.

'Thank you for our '*Zupa szczy*', says Jacek, a young Polish teenager, to the Russian serving out the soup.

The Poles around him burst into laughter. The laughter spreads and ripples through the queue and to others approaching, as more of them learn what he has said and they are all repeating it amongst themselves and laughing. The Russians take little notice, but must find it strange that their captives are so amused and so happy about the boiled water they have been given.

Jacek appropriately named the colourless, tasteless liquid, 'wee' or 'pee' soup. The Poles laugh at this. Zosia is amazed that any of them still have a sense of humour in the miserable circumstances they find themselves in. But they agree it is an extremely appropriate name, and it succeeds in bringing a smile to their faces. For most of them, it is the first time they have smiled or laughed since they left home.

Chapter 5

The elusive memory finally comes to her later that night. She is on her way to the market town of Storów with her father. It is late June, four months since her fifth birthday. The year is 1929 and the outing is a birthday treat, impatiently awaited.

As she and her father arrive in the market town of Storów, that is all forgotten. She cannot wait to see her friend Mila and explore the farmers' market with her. What will they find? What will they see?

Her father lifts her down from the tethered horse, kisses her on the cheek and smiles broadly. She adjusts the precious boater.

'You look lovely, my little one,' he says. 'Enjoy your special day.'

She beams at him.

He holds her hand as they walk down the paths and narrow lanes into the centre.

The lanes are bursting with people. The early birds are already leaving, walking towards them, carrying baskets of fruit and boxes full of vegetables. Many more people are making their way in to the town. Cows are being led down the narrow lanes. Boys are struggling to push carts loaded with all manner of things for sale.

'Hold on tightly, my love. Don't let go,' says her father. She squeezes his hand.

Zosia and her father thread through the bustling crowds, finally reaching the market square. Wide-eyed, she stares in amazement at the sight which opens up before her. She moves with her father into the cram-packed square, full of stalls, colour and noise.

'Beautiful blueberries, the freshest, juiciest you'll ever see! Picked this morning. Only 1 *złoty* a punnet,' shouts a stall holder.

'Rainbow tomatoes. Unripe, ripe, very ripe. All the colours of the rainbow, red, green, orange, yellow, take your pick,' shouts another.

Mounds of vegetables of all shapes and sizes, some of which she does not recognise, lie in heaps on the overfilled stalls. Surplus potatoes roll off and fall on the ground.

'We need to get to the other side of the square to find Mrs Tarkowska and Mila,' says Michał. 'Hold on tight. We'll go through the middle.'

They weave in and out of the stalls, forced to sample the sights and competing smells in the choked air. Musky pheasants, hang from curled, metal hooks. She has never seen dead pheasants, only live ones, creeping in and out of the bushes at the edge of the woods or flying overhead near her house. The smell of smoked cheeses mingles with the nutty smells of every variety of contorted mushroom. A sweet perfume rises from a stack of boxes, full of apples and brimming baskets of strawberries, her favourite fruit. A wall of colourful flowers floods the air with the scents of roses, lilies and peonies.

They manage to slip out through a gap, from the inner ring of stalls. No sooner does she take a breath, than the smell of warm, freshly baked bread, wafts past.

'Are you hungry Zosia?' says her father.

'Yes,'

'Shall we get some bread rolls with some cheese or honey?'

'Yes, honey please.'

She stands still for a moment as they wait for the rolls. She looks at the overflowing stalls. She has never seen anything like this.

'There is so much food here,' she thinks. 'There is enough to feed all the family for a very long time, and Mila's family, and Julcia's, and maybe even the whole of Bortków.'

She spots her favourite sweets nearby, '*Krówki*' (little cows) with a picture of a toffee-coloured cow on the wrapper.

'Please, please father, can I have some?' He buys her 200 grams. She is thrilled to receive the little paper bag filled with the delicious, caramel fudge sweets which melt on her tongue. He buys another bag for Mila.

They catch sight of Mila and her mother. Mrs Tarkowska is working on a stall selling home-baked cakes and pastries. The girls help on the stall, while Michał leaves to attend his official meeting.

A group of dancers and musicians in colourful costumes arrive in the square, arousing the interest of everyone. Like bees to a blossoming flower, sellers and passers-by swarm towards the spectacle and the noise of an accordion and drums. When the crowds have swelled sufficiently and the display has finished, one of the troupe shouts:

'Come to the show! Come and be amazed! You will not be disappointed. Do not miss it! 2 o'clock start.

'Please can we go, Mama,' says Mila. 'Please, Mrs Tarkowska,' says Zosia.

'Well, only if you come straight back as soon as it finishes.'

'We will, we promise,' says Mila.

Off they run to the field, not far from the centre, where the show is taking place. Bursting with excitement, they are carried along with the crowds, all heading to the same place. They manage to find one 'seat' among the straw bales laid out in front of the stage and squeeze together on the bale.

Act after entrancing act unfolds before their eyes. There are magicians, jugglers, actors, to name but a few. Acrobats 'fly' and somersault across the stage in sequined, turquoise leotards that sparkle in the sunlight. Twin clowns in identical harlequin-patterned costumes of magenta and bright lime, with conical hats, play tricks on the single Pierrot dressed in white from head to toe, except for a simple, black skull cap on his head encircling his sad, white-painted face. Will he outwit them or not? Zosia and Mila cannot stop laughing at their antics. Actors perform one of Aesop's Fables, 'The Boy Who Cried Wolf'. The girls join in with the audience when the boy is shouting and screaming to warn the villagers of the approaching wolf. A spellbinding tale of a knight and a princess follows. Then singers and dancers in national costume take to the stage. The final act invites the audience to join in on the field and the girls are more than happy to do so.

It is time for them to go back to Mila's mother. It seems to have become more crowded than earlier. People are pushing in all directions. The small girls find it difficult to see the way back. They are being engulfed by the crowd. Before they know it, they become separated, swept away from each other. Zosia finds herself in a maze of narrow streets which all look the same. They are full of clamour and people wearing masks and exotic costumes. A clown with a grotesque, painted smile comes up to her and tries to help, but scares her off instead. She runs away from him.

'Papa, Papa, save me,' she cries. But there is no reply.

She has lost all sense of direction and can't remember the way back. Nothing looks familiar. Her head is spinning. She starts to panic. Everything seems so big.

She is being drawn into a spiral of people, streets, noise, confusion. A feeling of helplessness overcomes her. She does not know which way to turn. The distorted, masked faces around her make everything a hundred times worse. Finally, she breaks down in tears. She sits down on a doorstep and cries. Streams of feet pass by her head. She can't see their faces.

'I'm lost. Papa, where are you? I'm lost.'

No one hears her. No one sees her. She stays there, not knowing what to do.

What seems like a long time later, amidst the endless clatter, she hears a tinkle of gold, her father's voice,

'Zosia! Zosia! where are you?'

'Papa! Over here!' she yells, again and again, but her tiny voice is lost in the din. She runs in the direction of his voice. She hears it again, the shiny, gold nugget on the drab, pebbled shore. But it is coming from the direction she has just come from. She turns back and is running towards it.

'Papa, Papa!' she calls. But she can no longer hear his voice.

'Papa! Where are you?' Then there is a total silence. As if in slow motion, she sees blotches of blackness floating in front of her eyes, which turn into a wall of blackness before she falls to the ground.

The next thing she hears is Mila's voice.

'Zosia, wake up, please wake up.' Her friend's muffled words reach her through a wave of what turns out to be very strong, smelling salts that Mila's mother is wafting under her nose. She sees them leaning over her, Mila's face joyous that Zosia has opened her eyes, and Mrs Tarkowska's relieved.

'You'll be alright now. Your father is looking for you too,' says Mrs Tarkowska.

Mila tells Zosia that she was also lost and has only just been reunited with her mother. When Zosia is able to stand up, Mila's mother takes them both back to the square and to Zosia's father whose eyes shine with tears when he sees her.

'Thank God, my little one,' he says.

He scoops her up into his arms, gives her a big kiss and hugs her tightly. How secure she feels in his warm embrace, how happy to be found and reunited with her dear father.

Chapter 6

Zosia's Journal

Autumn 1940

We've been here about six months. I don't know the date or what day of the week it is. All the days are the same. There is no day of rest. Sunday is just another work day here. Early on, when we thought it was Sunday, we sang hymns together and said prayers, like we did on the train. Now, most days, we pray in small groups or alone.

Juzef says that Autumn is short and cold, -20° degrees. Winter is longer and worse. He spares us any more details. I don't want to know how much longer and colder it is.

Terrible things are happening here. Many deportees in the camp are dying from sickness and starvation. Apart from stealing or foraging, there are no alternatives for us to get more food to help the sick survive. Stealing is not really an option. Who or where can we steal from? Not from each other. That would be unforgivable. In fact, the opposite is happening. Many of the captives are helping each other, often giving up their own rations to save loved ones and strangers in dire need.

Stealing from the soldiers? That is far too dangerous, even if anyone could work out a way to do it without being caught. The sack containing our rationed bread is a tempting target, but it is never left unattended, unless it's empty. Anyway, that would be stealing from ourselves. The guards would know immediately if the rations were short and everyone would be punished.

Foraging is useless for most of the year, as there is little in the forest that we can eat; nothing much grows under the metres of snow. Only the pine cones and berries can provide some nutrition and we continue to collect these and look for mushrooms whenever we can.

A few days ago, quite unexpectedly, our captors introduced a way for us to get increased rations that surprised all of us. It is a system they encourage. Anyone exceeding their daily quota of work by a certain amount, is able to get up to an extra 200 grams of bread a day. We can earn even more by exceeding our quota further. Everyone is desperate to do this. Of course, everyone is keen to work even harder, if it means they can get extra food.

Stronger deportees successfully exceed their quotas. They are giving their extra rations to weaker loved ones and to others who are sick. The Russians disapprove of this 'sharing', saying it is against the 'spirit' of the work ethic. But it doesn't stop the deportees from doing it.

A teenage boy, Benjamin, who was strong and worked hard, earned extra rations. Sara, his mother, was frail and sick. She was getting the basic ration, when she just managed to fulfil her quota. Ben could see that his mother was deteriorating and becoming weaker each day. She couldn't fulfil her quota anymore, so she didn't get any food. He gave her as much of the extra food and hot 'soup' as he could, but she was already suffering with bronchitis. One of the soldiers noticed that Ben was sharing his own rations with his mother.

They were both punished. The punishment was severe. Ben was put in a prison cell for a week in solitary confinement. He received nothing, except water. Sara could no longer work, so she got no rations. The deportees wanted to help her, they tried to smuggle food to her, but they couldn't get past the guards. They feared she would receive further punishment if they were found out. Sara was desperate to survive to see her son. Without medical attention, before the week was out, she wasted away alone, from her illness and from starvation.

When Ben was released from solitary and discovered that his mother had died, he was distraught. Despite being sick and emaciated by his ordeal, he had to work but was only given half rations for a further week. He became gravely ill with pneumonia and needlessly, Ben also died. No one had been able to help him, although many tried and very much wanted to, as they had with Sara, but it was impossible because the guards were watching him eagle-eyed day and night.

The Russians reward hard work and provide us with incentives. Everyone works as hard as they can just to get the essentials to survive: food and water. They work us extremely hard; far beyond our limits. I sometimes wonder if our captors are actually trying to kill off as many of us as they can. Why did they let Sara and Ben die? They could have prevented it. What did they gain by the unnecessary deaths of a mother and her teenage son?

When I asked Wojtek why they hadn't just shot us all in Poland and saved themselves the trouble of bringing us here, he said there would have been an outcry. This way they can just wear their prisoners down and work them to death. 'Who's counting? Who knows or cares about what's happening? Who even knew that they were there?' he said.

But why were they letting people die? He said it was because there was no death penalty in Russia. Besides, if what they were doing didn't work, the cold, disease or starvation would get us. That's what they do with 'enemies of the state,' which was what they said we were. I didn't really understand how we could be 'enemies of the state.' It was because the Russians said we were 'bourgeois, wealthy peasants,' and that made us 'enemies of the state'. I laughed. There is no such thing as a *wealthy* peasant. In the end, Wojtek said that everyone that the Russians imprison is classed an 'enemy of the state,' whoever they are.

I talked to my friend Karoline about it. She is in the same work group as me. She told me that the Russians had imprisoned some of their own people who they also called 'enemies of the state'. 'They were the 'ku'laks', imprisoned in labour camps where they worked hard until they died. It was 'The Great Terror' of the 1930s. She said that the barracks where we were living were built by those prisoners. I was surprised by how much she knew.

She told me that she had been studying History at the University of Lwów. She remembered reading about 'The Great Terror' in a book her professor showed the class. It was banned soon after the Russians invaded. It was her first year at the University. The war interrupted her studies.

Winter 1940 – Another day.
It is winter now. The temperature is -40° Celsius. We are snowed in. It has reached the top of the barracks. We have to dig the snow and clear a path in the mornings to get our rations and to get to the carts for work.

The soles of the boots I had on when I left Poland have worn through in several places. The holes let in the cold. The wet ice seeps in as soon as I step out of the barracks in the morning. There is no way of drying the shoes or my feet. All day I work with my feet sodden and cold. It is utterly miserable and before long I get bronchitis. I'm not the only one at all.

A deportee, called Tomas, is going to speak to the Russians about the spread of bronchitis. Increasingly more children are getting ill and the elderly are dying. We are using scraps of old newspapers we find in the soldiers' bins to put in our shoes to stop the water and cold reaching our feet. This is small comfort. It works in part and only for a short time until the paper itself is wet through. But it is better than nothing, as it staves off the cold and wet for part of the morning.

But one morning, there were no newspapers in the bins. I went back to the barracks. The thought of all day without any respite from cold, wet feet was hard to bear. Genia tried to help but she had nothing that I could use. Wojtek dug in his coat pockets and pulled out a few crumpled pages of newspaper and gave them to me.

I was so grateful and relieved. There were only three pages of the newspaper, not quite enough for my purpose, but it would do. I unfolded it to start wrapping it around my feet.

A separate cutting which looked like it was from a different paper, fell out from between the pages. A cartoon on it caught my eye.

It was a picture of a large, fat bear and a wolf in military uniform attacking a group of sad-looking, helpless sheep. The bear had a hammer and sickle in its paws and a Russian flag was draped around its neck. The wolf was holding a German flag and its face was that of a man whose name was inscribed on a badge on his collar, A. Hitler. Behind them there was a map of Poland on a wall. It was ripped in half from north to south.

The caption under the cartoon read: 'The brave bear and the ravenous wolf divide the sheep between them.'

On the front page of the main newspaper, the headline read:

'Nazis, Soviets Sign Pact; Hitler Tells Britain It's 'Too Late' for Peace; All Europe Arms!'[1]

What was this 'Pact'? It's the first I'd heard of it. No one had talked about this. The article said that a Treaty of Friendship, known as the Ribbentrop-Molotov Pact was signed in Moscow on the 23rd August 1939. It was a ten-year Non-Aggression Pact between Germany and the Soviet Union. In an accompanying, 'secret' document, the common interest of dividing Poland between themselves was agreed. The division was to be along the Curzon Line, a line running the length of Poland from north to south.

I couldn't believe it. This had happened before the Germans invaded at the beginning of September. They had a plan and an agreement to divide Poland between themselves, before any invasion had taken place.

The third page was from another newspaper.[2] In one of the articles, Russia claimed that it was their duty 'to extend the hand of brotherly assistance to White Russian and Ukrainian peoples' in Poland and 'to bring the Polish peoples out of the misery into which they have been plunged.' But this seemed to contradict their pact of friendship with Germany.

After all this time, over a year and two months, everything was finally clear. The agreement between Germany and Russia before they both invaded was stated in black and white. The motives of the Russian invasion were confirmed. The confusion and the doubts anyone may have had early on, were over. Adam was right. Władysław and Urszula were right. They would have known this before the deportation started. It helped to explain why they had felt so desperate about what might happen. I don't know how they managed to get these papers. A relative or friend must have given them or sent them from America.

How long had Wojtek known? I remember how his expression altered when he read the newspaper that Władysław gave him on the train. Now I understand why. But why had he not said a word about it? It was a long time ago, months ago. The day we changed trains at the Russian border was when Władysław gave him the newspaper. He had kept it secret from us all this time. Perhaps he was trying to protect us from the terrible truth of what was really happening. I didn't put the newspaper pages in my boots. I folded them carefully and put them in my journal.

Winter, – Monday perhaps?

I name the days, to try and count the weeks.

Whatever Tomas had said to the soldiers must have worked. The Russians introduced '*sapogi*'. These were boots, made of leather, with thick, rubber soles and were lined with wool; harsh to the touch, but warm, and most importantly, dry. Everyone was desperate to have them, to put an end to the endless cold, wet misery we had been putting up with. The boots instantly became prized possessions. But, typically of the regime, they were not given out freely to everyone, or to those who needed them most. They had to be earned. Only those who succeeded in exceeding their work quotas on a daily basis for a whole week could get the boots. Nothing was ever given freely, even though we had been forcibly exiled from our homeland and had everything taken from us. The strict work ethic had to be followed. We had to work even harder to get the boots. Some of us got the boots. But some died in their attempts.

By then, so many were weak and weary that fulfilling their quota was becoming an impossible task. It was a never-ending vicious circle. Less or no food and no dry shoes could not result in better and more efficient workers. Escalating numbers were affected by illness, disease and death.

The regime and conditions were brutal. The military precision of the soldiers in assessing quotas and distributing rations, obsessive. At the end of every morning and evening, they checked the quota of work.

They would count everything. They counted the felled trunks and recorded the number in their notebooks. If the number was not high enough, there was no extra bread, and no chance at all of the boots, just more prolonged suffering and misery.

We were stuck in this frustrating deadlock.

* * *

Zosia and Karoline were warming themselves by the fire outside the barrack in the evening when they overheard Tomas talking to a couple of deportees. They were talking about what the soldiers did when they counted the felled trunks. They had observed that the soldiers marked the end of each one with an indelible mark to indicate it had been counted and to ensure there was no chance of it being counted again by mistake.

The guard counted and marked the trunks in the morning. He recorded the numbers of felled trunks. The process was repeated at the end of the working day to count the trunks felled by the end of the late afternoon.

'There must be a way we can somehow increase our quotas without actually doing so,' said Maciek, one of Tomas's group.

'You mean, cheat the quota,' said Danka.

'Yes, if that's what you want to call it. For many it is impossible to even fulfil their quotas. They're dying. It's a matter of life and death.'

'We need to find a way to outsmart them.' said Danka.

'I've been thinking,' said Tomas. 'You've seen how when they count the felled trunks, they mark the end of each trunk with an indelible mark.'

'Yes, they're very careful. They never miss any out,' said Danka.

'What we need to do is find a way to somehow remove that mark.'

'How can we do that? They use an indelible marker. It would be easy if it was chalk,' said Maciek.

'Well, they're not stupid, are they,' said Danka.

'No. But there must be a way. If we could think of a way to remove the mark,' said Maciek.

There was a long pause. They sat warming themselves round the fire, watching the heap of burning twigs and branches. They stared into the fire, listening to its hissing and spitting.

'I've got it!' said Tomas. 'If we cut off the mark, cut off the end of the trunk with the mark on it, then the guards would count the trunk again.'

'Won't they realise it's the same trunk they counted in the morning?'

But Tomas had an answer to Maciek's question.

'Not if we move it to a different place to fool them. The morning logs are usually rolled down to the river side or logged down to the mill by midday. If we move it to another place, they'll assume the ones they'd marked earlier had gone, and that this was a new one they hadn't marked yet.'

'That's brilliant, but how exactly do we cut off the end of the trunks without being seen? And how do we dispose of them without being caught?' said Danka.

'Okay, we need to work out the details of how we can do it. It won't be easy but if we succeed, we can increase the quota and you know what that means,' said Tomas.

Word of the plan spread through the ranks of the deportees involved in felling the trees and transporting the logs. Those interested and with any ideas were to make contact.

Karoline and Zosia went to speak to Tomas and his friends about the ingenious idea.

'I'll do it. I know how we can do it,' said Zosia.

'Me too,' said Karoline.

'When we've finished sawing off all the branches of a log, we wait till it is marked and then when the soldiers go for their lunch break, we can sneak back.'

Karoline added: 'If there is any problem, we can use the pretext of sawing off more branches or clearing the ground or some other excuse.'

'And then using our handsaws, we saw off a thin sliver of wood, with the mark on it, from the end of the trunk,' Zosia said.

'Good, that's good. But it's going to be very dangerous, and we need to dispose of the evidence,' said Danka.

'We can't get caught. We'll use lookouts, to warn if any soldiers are coming,' added Tomas.

'We can hide the bit we've sawn off in our pockets, if we chop it up into pieces. Then we can burn them together with the small branches we've officially cut off earlier,' said Zosia.

'Right, we need a group of you to do the sawing off, and a group of lookouts,' said Tomas.

Journal continued, Winter, – Monday perhaps?
The idea was simple and, if successful, could be very effective in getting us out of the dreadful deadlock we were in. We would potentially double our quotas which would mean more food and *sapogi* for more of us. More of us would have a chance of being saved.

But Tomas had said, we needed to make sure that the soldiers did not suspect we were up to anything. Too much increase in the quota would be suspicious. We had to do it very gradually, intermittently and also taking into account the circumstances each day. Some days would be easier than others. There might be fewer soldiers. We would have to wait for them to go for their lunch break at the same time. Some days we could be in an area of forest that provided more screening than usual and other helpful factors. We would have to assess and plan carefully. If we were caught, the consequences would be unthinkable. The punishment severe.

A few days later Karoline, myself and the other girls who worked sawing off the branches of the felled trees, received word that an attempt to carry out the plan was to take place.

'This is it Zosia,' said Karoline. 'Are you ready?'

Yes, I was. I certainly was ready and eager.

When the soldiers left for lunch and we had the signal that all was clear, a small group of deportees spread out in the forest forming a chain. They took it in turns to keep a look out for the comings and goings of the soldiers. They could pass messages down the chain. We had an emergency signal: an owl hoot, if danger was near.

My friends and I ran down to where the marked trunks lay. We could see the last look out, who signalled again that all was clear. My heart was beating fast, my hands were shaking. I tried to saw the end of the trunk off. I looked up to check the look out again.

'Come on Zosia, stop looking around. Just get on with it,' said Karoline. She held the trunk steady.

I was trying. From that moment the saw seemed to glide through the wood and detach the marked end cleanly. We chopped it up into small pieces and put it in our coat pockets. Karoline cut the second trunk. We managed to do two trees. We were only to do one or two at most, as it was the first attempt and in order not to arouse suspicion. A few of the girls stood further down the trunk, to make it look as if they were sawing off some remaining small branches on the trunks. We ran back and put the evidence on the fire along with the branches, we had sawn off earlier.

When we finished, the 'new' trunks were rolled to a different position for the soldiers to count again in the afternoon. We watched them counting the prepared trunks again and marking them again.

Eureka! I celebrated silently in my heart without betraying any outward sign of joy. A tiny win over our oppressors. But it felt like a huge victory. And it was. Success meant 200 grams more bread or *sapogi* for one or two of us. Each day we succeeded, we felt triumphant.

Within a few weeks 'Tomas's ploy' as we called it, or 'Cheating the Quota' made it possible for the weakest to get what they needed: an increase in their level of survival and some basic human essentials. For many, it proved to be the difference between survival and death. We are going to continue doing this for as long as we absolutely can.

Chapter 7

The searing cold cuts through Zosia as she climbs on to the trailer. That day she is not with Karoline and her usual group, and not with Juzef on his cart. The rusty, old trailer, pulled by two horses, can take about twenty at a time standing in the back. It takes them a long way into the depths of the forest to a part none of them have been to before.

At the work point, the soldiers disperse them into different areas. They single out particular trees and order them to saw off the lower branches. For once, Zosia is alone. There are a few other lone workers not too far off doing the same. The last time she was on her own was a long time ago, somewhere on a sun-filled hilltop overlooking distant cornfields, before the deportation. The isolation provided by the forest seems strange. A sense of vulnerability creeps up on her. But being away from the ever-present eyes of the soldiers is liberating.

Freedom is a dream. Any notion of escape is out of the question. The few that have tried it are inevitably caught and punished. They die as a result of the prolonged solitary confinement in a dark cell, with almost no food or water. Those who are not caught, perish in the snows. There is no place of safety to escape to for hundreds of miles.

The sawn branches are stacked in piles for the trailer. The forest silence is interrupted by the sound of voices laughing and joking in Russian. Their voices grow louder as they get nearer. There are two of them, Russian soldiers. They are walking towards her, grinning at her. A shiver passes through her. Where are the other workers? How could she be so stupid, to stay isolated from them? But those were her orders.

'Well, what have we here?' says one of the soldiers.

'A pretty one, I'd say,' says the other one.

'Let's have a closer look. Take off your coat, girl.'

Zosia remains still for a moment. Their motives are clear. The handsaw lying on the ground is her only defence.

'Take off your coat.'

Slowly, she begins to remove her coat. As she lifts her arms out of her coat, she unexpectedly throws it at the soldier's face, with the aim of slowing him down. She picks up the handsaw, turns and runs as fast as she can into the forest. Unburdened, free of her coat, she is light and fast. They are shouting angrily and coming after her, in their heavy army uniforms and thick, winter long-coats. She runs until she has no more breath. She slides into a dip in the ground and hides herself behind a fallen trunk. She lies there trembling, panting. She can hear them coming. They are getting nearer. Her heart is pounding, beating fast against her chest. She prays that they will not see her and they will give up and go back.

'What chance do I have? There's two of them.' She still has the handsaw. She will use it to defend herself. They are approaching fast. She tries to hold her breath but that only makes it worse. She manages to regain her breath and is breathing steadily. She remains perfectly still. She can see one of them through the trees. His boots about five or six metres away.

Behind her, a faint crackle, like the fall of a drop of melting ice on a dry leaf, alerts her to the possibility of danger. Without turning around, she senses a presence behind her. The almost imperceptible sound of steady breathing, and a stream of breath flowing past in the periphery of her line of vision paralyse her with fear. Another crackle. This time it is the sound of a footstep moving towards her. Is it the other soldier coming up behind her?

Rigid with fear, terrified of facing the danger. Another footstep. She spins round. There face to face with her, stands a huge, dark wolf. Its head and shoulders are lowered and it is baring its teeth. Then even more threateningly, it starts producing a low, rumbling growl.

The wolf is motionless, its growl growing greater and more threatening. The thick, matted fur on its back moves up and down with every breath. Although it is huge, it is skinny, scrawny and worst of all, there is no doubt, it is starving. Its growl continues to grow. The soldiers keep very still. They do not have their rifles with them. They would have shot it dead.

'Let's get out of here. Leave her to the wolf,' one of them says.

At that moment, the wolf makes its move. It leaps on to the soldier, attacking his arm and then his leg. Blood is spurting out of his hand. He has gashes on his leg where the wolf has ripped through his trousers. The soldier is screaming in agony. The other soldier is trying to scare the wolf off his friend, but the wolf is vicious. He attacks him too injuring him on his face. Blood is pouring from his nose and he has a large cut on his forehead from the wolf's claw. He starts running away.

'I'll get the rifles,' he says, holding onto his face and leaving his compatriot on the ground.

'Wait, help me. Help me to stand up.' But he has already gone.

Zosia knows that her immediate instinct to turn and run is futile. There is no way she will be able to outrun the wolf. If she doesn't move, he might lose interest in her and disappear back into the thickness of the forest. If she runs, he will definitely pounce on her.

For the briefest of moments, the wolf shudders but continues to remain unmoving. She looks at the terrifying animal, its eyes meet hers. They stare directly at each other. There is no doubt that any moment he will pounce on her. She is still holding the handsaw and is ready to use it in self-defence. Should she make the first move and surprise the wolf or is it better to wait and see what the wolf does and then strike in self-defence? The wolf lowers its head, level with its shoulders and lets out a low, rumbling growl. The moment stretches out like a long tunnel into the distance.

'Cick,ts,ya!' the driver of the trailer shouts, as he cracks his whip near the horses. Instantly, the wolf vanishes into the enveloping vastness of the forest.

The wolf's plight is similar to hers. Neither of them has much control over their existence in this forsaken place. They are both just scraping to survive. Fear of what is to come is increasing.

Speechless, shaken, she gets on to the trailer.

'Is this your coat?' says the driver. She holds out her hand and takes it from him.

'It was left near the trailer. One of the workers brought it back from the forest. I thought something must be wrong. No one ever takes their coat off here and leaves it.'

She is more thankful than he will ever know.

The other workers have all gone. She rides back on the empty trailer. How lucky that the driver appeared in time. She must have been seconds away from being attacked by the wolf. What would have happened if the wolf hadn't appeared and the soldiers had caught her?

She slumps down on the floor of the trailer. Looking up to the heavens, she thanks God for saving her. The last shred of daylight closes-in like a shroud.

The trailer rocks her from side to side over the uneven ground. In no time at all, she enters her other world. Memories fill her head. She is riding on the horse with her father through the cornfields. She loses her hat. He is waist deep in the corn as she waits for him. She knows he will return with it. He encloses her in his arms, as they ride together on the horse. She is safe.

She is safe in the glorious days of harvest time and the endless playing in the cornflower and poppy-dotted meadows, of running free among the hills and along the sun-glistening streams. The long, lazy bee-buzzing afternoons of harvesting, when Mila, Julcia and her bring round drinks and cakes for the workers. In the late evening, the lingering heat of the departing sun proudly parades and spreads out the magnificence of its crimson, glowing gown across the evening horizon, to the playing of music, followed by singing and dancing.

'It is my other world, the one stolen from us, my other time and place.'

Her hat is tossed by the wind onto the field. From its red ribbon a droplet of blood falls, then another, until there is a scattering of tiny droplets. A small spot appears in the corner of the field. It begins to grow, staining the perfect tablecloth of the field.

The trailer stops with a sharp jerk. It brings her back to the present. They are back at the Camp. Her reminiscing of home is shattered, as abruptly as the forced departure had been.

'Off the trailer! Get down!' shouts the driver. But she cannot move. She is stuck. She has no sensation in her feet. Her face is achingly numb. It is worse when she tries to speak, to call out to the driver for help. 'Come on, out!' he says.

Juzef is standing there. He must be waiting for their return, to help with the horses. He looks concerned when he sees her and rushes over. Before she knows it, he is scooping up handfuls of snow and is rubbing it vigorously on her cheeks, but she feels nothing.

'Quick Alex! She's frozen up! It's frostbite!' he says to his son. 'Rip her *sapogi* off and rub her feet and legs as fast as you can.' Alex does as he is told and so the two of them rub snow on her face and feet for a good half hour to restore the blood flow. Her cheeks are rigid. As they rub, she begins to feel some sensation returning to her body. The frostbite is severe. It must have started when she was on the trailer. She was not fully conscious, maybe she was asleep, not moving and daydreaming on the way back.

The young man is succeeding in restoring some feeling to her feet and legs. He looks up at her and smiles. Of course, she recognises him. The frozen coma is beginning to thaw. Close-up, she sees his clear green eyes, enhanced with flecks of amber – intriguing, translucent pools as inviting as an iridescent lake in summer and a smile as warm as the midsummer sun.

Slowly the sensations return to her face and feet. Her face aches, the muscles in her legs ache. Juzef tells her that it will need more time to completely return to normal. She produces what passes for a smile for her rescuers, and for one of them, in particular.

Chapter 8

Late that evening, Zosia is sat warming herself by the fire outside the barracks. Karoline is walking towards her.

'Hey Zosia, what are you doing staring into the fire? Where were you today? We missed you.' Karoline sits down next to her friend. Zosia tells her what happened in the forest and about the frostbite.

'A lot has happened today. My feet and face are almost back to normal. But not my heart?'

'What do you mean?' says Karoline.

She doesn't tell Karoline about Alex. It's her secret, for now.

'Do you think we'll ever get back home from here? It's so far, it's impossible. Would it ever be the same? They have taken our homes and stolen our lives from us, it breaks my heart,' says Zosia.

'I don't know if we'll ever get back. But we have to focus on the here and now, on surviving, that's all we can do. Be strong and survive. Who knows what's going to happen?'

Karoline cheers her up a little.

'What do you miss the most?' says Zosia.

'My family. But, as you know, they were taken prisoner by the Germans and put on a train headed west, to Germany, I suppose. I was only left behind because I was at the University that day. When I got home in the evening, they were all gone.'

Zosia puts her arm round her friend and hugs her.

'I miss my family the most too. The fire reminds me of us all sitting round the hearth,' says Zosia. Karoline stares into the fire.

'Family, they are so precious,' says Karoline. 'Nothing can replace them.'

She wipes the tears from her face with the sleeve of her coat. They sit staring into the fire huddled together. After a while, Karoline says,

'You're right though Zosia, they have stolen our lives. I miss being at university. I loved it, all that learning, all those clever people. The first year was so interesting. I don't know if I'll ever be able to go back, but that's my dream.'

'We need our dreams, especially here,' says Zosia, 'and our memories.' She continues:

'Today getting frostbite, Juzef and his son ripping off my *sapogi* and rubbing my feet and face reminds me of the first time I had frostbite.

I was four years old. I remember it was around Christmas time. The snow looked like rolled out cotton wool. There were mounds of snow piled up against the wall of the barn and against the side of the house where it had blown in. The lake on the farmstead was frozen. We all wanted to go skating on it. My older brothers had been sent out to measure how deep the ice was. It was more than half a metre thick, so it was safe.

We all went skating, my friends, Mila and Julcia and my brothers. Julcia's eighteen-year-old sister, Mariola came to look after us. My mother was ill, she couldn't go out. Father and my oldest brother were out tending to the animals and bringing in any lost cattle or trapped sheep. Sometimes sheep got caught in the wire fences and couldn't get free if their coats got tangled up in the barbed wire.

The ice was so thick on the lake, that there was no danger of anyone falling in. What we hadn't realised was that the main threat was not falling in, but the freezing temperatures. It was -10 degrees Celsius. We didn't even have proper skates then. We were out in our normal winter boots. To keep our feet warm, we had put on as many pairs of woollen socks as it was possible to squeeze into the boots. Julcia's cheeks were red raw with cold and Mila's teeth chattered but we were happy and excited.

We ran across the crisp snow down to the lake. I felt the first snow seep over the top of my boots. I didn't pay attention to it apart from the shock of the initial sensation as it reached my feet. The fun of skating on the lake completely took over. Nothing else mattered. We slid about on the ice like clumsy ducklings on a pond, weaving and dancing around, sliding and racing each other from one side of the lake to the other. We were almost the only ones on the ice. A few children and young people from the village had joined us. We stayed there for a long time, losing all track of time. It must have been several hours. We had got used to falling over and getting up on the ice. Mariola said that the secret was not to be afraid of falling over, and we weren't. The more times we fell over, the better we became and the more confident we grew. But then I fell over and I couldn't get up. My feet felt numb. I shouted to Kazik and to Mariola to help me.

'I can't feel my feet, I can't move them!' I remember shouting. Mariola must have realised what had happened. She asked me if I could wriggle my toes, I couldn't, I couldn't even feel them.

Kazik and Mariola hurriedly carried me to the edge of the lake where we had left a small sledge. They lifted me on to it and pulled it back through the snow. Mila and Julcia were running alongside. When we got home, Kazik carried me into the house and put me down on the hearth, in front of the roaring fire.

By this time, I was in agony. My mother came down to see what was causing all the noise. She must have known what the problem was immediately. She told my brother to pull off my boots and socks and asked Kasia to bring some butter from the kitchen and put it near the fire.

They removed my wet boots and the layers of soaked socks. I couldn't feel my feet. They were like blocks of ice. My mother started rubbing the softened butter on my feet. They took it in turns to rub my feet and calves.

Mother asked Kasia to heat up some soup in the kitchen and bring it in for everyone. After what seemed like about an hour of rubbing, I began to feel some sensation in my toes. It spread slowly through my feet and up my calves. The circulation was returning. The hot, steaming soup and the glowing heat of the crackling fire helped to warm me up. They continued rubbing my legs until Mother was satisfied. When they stopped, she covered me with a soft blanket. I must have fallen asleep in front of the fire.

I woke up to the smell of hot food. Kasia was bringing in some hot beef and vegetable stew with potatoes, followed by one of her delicious apple cakes for everyone. I remember the sight of my friends and family listening to my mother reading a story about Aladdin from one of her books, 'The Book of One Thousand and One Nights, The Arabian Nights'. I listened to the hypnotic tale of magic lamps and magic carpets in far off, snowless lands. We loved listening to stories. I looked round and saw their Botticelli, rosy-cheeked faces shining in the candlelight and in the glinting reflections from the decorations on the Christmas tree.'

'I love listening to your stories, Zosia,' says Karoline.

In the barrack that night, Zosia lies awake. Thoughts of her childhood are eclipsed by new ones rising in her mind. 'Alex' is his name. His broad smile and the way he looks at her, stir overpowering feelings deep within her like she has never experienced before.

Chapter 9

Zosia's Journal

May 1941

Days have gone by, weeks have gone by. It is ages since I last saw Alex. I don't know what to do. Something may have happened to him. Should I ask his father? No. Juzef would probably think it strange if I showed any concern about Alex. But it's been such a long time.

What I need to do is just stop thinking about Alex, and his mesmerising green eyes and his enticing smile – and just forget about him. Yes, that's it. That's decided. That's what I need to do. *Forget about him.*

* * *

Zosia shuts her notebook firmly, puts it together with her pen, in her bag, places it under the bed and walks out of the barrack. The rest of the family left for the meeting point before her. She was pleased to have a few minutes on her own in the barrack to think.

Antoni is far too heavy to carry now, besides he is walking and running. Genia likes them all to go down together. The children run on ahead while Wojtek and her can have a moment to talk. Zosia looks for them along the path, but cannot see them.

She reaches the clearing in time for the daily orders. Her sister and family are there standing in line. She joins them. The orders are the same as the day before and the day before that: the same work, the same group, the same cart, but not the same quota. The quotas have been increased. It is not the first time. There is no choice. Everyone will have to do more work for the same rations. The family disperses.

Zosia looks around for Tomas, Danka or Maciek, hoping for some sign that they will be planning another attempt at 'cheating the quota.' Instead, she sees *him*, Alex, striding towards the line of carts waiting to take the deportees to the work stations. He stops at one of the carts, strokes the horses and is climbing up onto the driver's seat.

Juzef's cart is a little further on from Alex's. She will have to walk past Alex. He is looking at her. As she gets nearer, she can feel her heart beating faster. He smiles at her, she smiles back. The feelings she had decided to put out of her mind that morning are deeply stirred. How could she *'Forget about him?'*

Chapter 10

'Karoline, I've got something I want to tell you,' says Zosia.

'It'll have to wait,' says Karoline. 'This is really important. It's a matter of life and death. Can you swim, Zosh?'

'No.'

'Well, I'll have to teach you.'

'Why? I don't want to swim… in ice-cold water,' says Zosia.

'But my dear friend, you will probably have to, to save your life.'

Zosia's Journal –June-July 1941, 'Ice turns to Water'
I slept uneasily thinking about Karoline's words. I hate that question. About swimming. It brings back tortuous memories.

The metre-thick layers of ice on the hard, Siberian river are thawing and the snow is receding fast. Translucent drops of ice sparkle in the faintest glimmer of sunlight and fall gently, like silent tears landing on the softening cheek of the earth.

I wake earlier than usual, before five o'clock, and lie there thinking. Everyone is still asleep. The children look like little angels; grubby, thin, pale-faced angels, not the chubby, rosy-cheeked ones on Christmas cards.

It was still too cold to get up, I huddled with the cherubs. Around 6.00am, Genia starts to stir. I get up and slip outside. I break the thinning skin of ice on the bucket, splash a handful of cold water on my face and collect my ration. I eat the self-prescribed, one-half of rationed bread, put the rest of it in my pocket and drink a cup of tepid boiled water.

It is a year and four months since we were forced out of our homes. We have grown used to the regimented routine: the impoverished diet, the freezing temperatures, and the almost nonexistent, blurred glimpse of a sullen, withdrawn sun locked away behind a wall of cloud.

Juzef drives the horse and cart as far into the dark depths of the inexhaustible forests as we can penetrate to transport the logs which we have been cutting down, preparing and stacking up the previous day. In the frozen ten months of winter, we rolled the logs onto the ice and slid them downstream to the mill, running alongside the logs on the ice and pushing them with an oar-like pole.

Now, it is June, 'summer' as they call it. Our second, 'long, glorious Siberian summer!' that Juzef jokes about. The summer we've been waiting for.

But summer means we will have to transport the logs on a moving river, much more precarious, especially, if you can't swim. Somehow, we didn't have to do this the first summer, but Karoline is sure we will this year.

* * *

Zosia remembers the conversation with Karoline a few days earlier.

'Listen Zosh. It's easy,' she said. 'All you need to remember is to kick your legs and move your arms through the water, like this.' She mimed the arm and leg movements for breaststroke and then for front crawl, counting out the rhythm of the strokes.

'Karoline, I…' *I knew I would have to tell her.*

'What is it Zosh?'

'I..I had a very bad experience when I was seven. I… nearly drowned. I never learned to swim after that, and… I haven't told anyone…but I am terrified of water. I can't even go in.'

Journal

I know she desperately wants to help me. We both know the Russian work ethic: only those who fulfil their work quota get their rations. Now, I would have to overcome my fear and lumberjack on the river if I wanted to survive. I remember the promise I made to my parents, not to give up, to do everything to survive.

We practise the swimming strokes on land as the days grow longer and perceptibly warmer.

'Be brave. Just do it!' I tell myself, every time I come near the water. But no matter how hard Karoline tries to help and no matter how much I want to overcome my fear, I am trapped in the pincer-tight grip of my phobia. She's right. If I don't overcome it, I will die.

We get to the forest work base by 7.00 am and work starts with the sharp whistle of the soldier in charge and the usual abrupt orders. The dark flow of water is clearly visible. It is menacing, a shadowy underwater monster lurking beneath the surface.

Karoline told me I'd be fine, to enjoy it, to imagine the logs are dolphins that I was riding on. If I fall off, all I had to do was to just grab on to one of the dolphins.

Karoline is fearless. She is one of the first to go, standing triumphantly astride two logs and controlling them with her thick, oar-like pole. I watch her in admiration gliding across the mercurial surface. She makes it look so easy.

She is heading for a turning in the river and about to disappear out of sight. Then quite unexpectedly, a shout. I can see her arms waving about as she loses her balance and falls off the logs into the river. The 'dolphins' float away. She is swimming towards the edge. She is making slow progress, the weight of her heavy clothes and bulky boots are dragging her down.

I start running towards her. Others follow, egging her on and running to help. A couple of the young soldiers run with us.

She is trying to take her weighty coat off to make it easier to swim. She manages to stay afloat for long enough to peel it off. It is snatched away by the hungry river. She is swimming more quickly now and getting closer to the shore, out of the main current of the river. I am well ahead of the others, about twenty yards away from her and I can see her face clearly. Her expression shows that it is not easy. She looks like she is having to use all her strength to swim, every last breath.

Without any warning, her expression changes from one of agonising effort, to one of sheer terror, as she sees a whirlpool in front of her opening up its gapping jaws. She cannot avoid it, the river is pulling her along. Her arms are thrashing about wildly, she is screaming and telling me to get back. But I can't stand by and do nothing. I run into the water, throwing in a couple of large branches for Karoline to grab hold of. But they are swallowed up by the whirlpool. I wade out further, to as far up to the edge of the whirlpool as possible, throwing her my coat so she can grasp it and then I can pull her out by it. She stretches her hand out for it but can't reach it. I look at her across the whirlpool, Karoline is screaming and desperately trying to swim. The most terrifying sight follows. In a split second, she vanishes from sight. Underwater. Swallowed whole in one gulp by the greedy river, dragged down into the depths of its belly. The force of the whirlpool far too great for her to overcome. It is not even possible to recover her body from the treacherous waters.

I am numb, looking for her in the water, praying she will surface further down the river, any moment. All I can see is Karoline's terrified face and her last words trying to protect me, telling me to get back. My dearest friend. I have lost my dearest friend. What a tragic waste of her young life.

Later that same day, I stand trance-like on two logs and through bitter, salty tears streaming down my face, stunned by Karoline's senseless death, I feel the cool river breeze and the swollen belly of the river under my feet, gurgling and transporting me as I sail towards the sawmill.

'Take me too. If you don't swallow me, I'll starve to death here anyway.'

Chapter 11

Zosia's Journal

July-August 1941

I miss Karoline so much. Since her drowning, I haven't been able to sleep properly. Lying awake at night, I see the bulky river heaving and swirling treacherously towards the mills. I see Karoline struggling to escape being devoured by the perilous whirlpool. I see her terrified face in the final moment before she disappears. Why God, why? I can't understand it. I cry silently. I do not want to wake the others and I do not want the children to hear or see.

She was only nineteen. She was the first, but not the last. More deportees are drowning every day, helpless against the forces of the treacherous river. I try to make sense of why we are even here and why any of this is happening. I don't have any answers.

'Thy will be done on earth as it is in heaven.'

The young soldiers moored a kayak along the river today to provide some help to anyone in difficulty on the river. If only they had done this sooner.

The tragedy of Karoline's drowning has made me determined to overcome the river. My fear of water seemed to disappear when I was trying to save Karoline. I didn't think about getting into the water. I just went straight in to save her.

I wish I had managed to tell Karoline about Alex. She would have loved to hear about him. Alex is the only thing that is keeping me from despair in this deathly place.

That day when I arrived back at the barracks, wet from floating the logs downstream, from the cart I could see that Alex was there. He was helping with the horses, unhooking them from the carts. He turned around. When he saw me, he smiled and walked towards me.

He could see that I was upset and asked me what was wrong. I told him about the drowning.

'Come with me,' he said, gently. I followed.

He unhooked the horses from the cart and led them to the stables.

Seeing that I was wet, he got a blanket, put it on my shoulders and wrapped it round me. We sat down on a small wooden bench in the stables. I told him about Karoline and her drowning. There was a deep sadness in his eyes.

'Losing someone close, someone you love is perhaps the hardest thing to bear, I know,' he said. He told me about his mother who died when he was twelve. Juzef had been a widower for the past eight years. We talked about our families and about our homes for a long time. I told him about my parents.

He asked me if I was cold, but talking to Alex and wrapped in the blanket, I had completely forgotten about being wet or cold.

'Hey, Alexander! Come quickly and help with the horses outside!' shouted his boss.

The moment ended.

Chapter 12

From the cart, Juzef leans down and hands Zosia a small sealed envelope.

'It's for you,' he says. '*What could it be?*'

She climbs into the back of the cart. Standing in a corner, she opens it carefully. It is a letter. '*Who could be sending me a letter?*' It is from Alex.

Dear Zosia,

How are you? I hope you are alright and haven't caught a cold after getting wet on the river and sitting in the cold stables.

I hope you don't mind me writing to you. I wasn't sure when or how I could communicate with you, as I'm not going to be in the camp until next week.

I am back in my family home. It's over twenty kilometres away, and I haven't been able to be at the camp again since I last saw you.

The day I first saw you, when you'd broken your leg, I had been called by the officer in charge at the camp to come and repair the electricity in the soldiers' quarters. I took advantage of being there to see my father, as he stays up at the camp most days in the winter. As you know the daylight hours are short, so it makes sense for him to stay there, rather than make the long journey through the snow in the dark every day.

Now I come up whenever they need me to help.

Zosia, I was wondering if perhaps we could meet. I will be at the camp again, next Thursday, a week from today. Can we meet then? Maybe after you finish your work shift. If you agree and if it's possible, meet me behind the medical barrack when you get back. I'll be waiting for you.

Love,
Alex

'Love, Alex,' she repeats to herself. The feelings she had when she first saw Alex well up inside her. She kisses the letter surreptitiously, folds it and slips it back into its envelope and into her coat pocket. Inwardly, she is laughing and crying at the same time.

From that moment, she is just waiting for Thursday afternoon to arrive. A week, seven whole days. It seems an eternity away.

Chapter 13

Zosia's Journal, Thursday

At last, it is the day I am to meet him.

I work hard in a kind of daze on the day Alex is coming, sawing off the branches more quickly, collecting up the branches more quickly, as if doing things more quickly will somehow make the time to the end of the shift arrive sooner. Outdoing my quota without realizing, because the only thing that matters to me now is seeing Alex at the end of the shift. I don't even think about being hungry, about eating or not eating.

When I get back to camp, I make my way to the medical centre. I try to tidy my hair, my hands are shaking. Embarrassed about my shabby and dirty appearance, I run to the water butt and splash my face with cold water. I see him, and all this is forgotten. Alex is there, waiting behind the medical building. He smiles and starts walking towards me. He looks at me the way he looked at me the first time we saw each other.

'Shall we go for a walk?' he says.

We walk into the woods, moving further and further into its depths. We manoeuvre through the tightly packed trees, once, brushing close against each other. He catches my hand. A frisson of excitement ignites. His smile irresistibly draws me to him. He pulls me close gently, looking into my eyes, then at my lips, and kisses me cautiously, as if I might break. The cautiousness lasts just a few seconds longer. Our feelings explode and we are now kissing passionately. I have never felt like this.

'Zosia, I…I can't stop thinking about you,' he says. 'Since I first saw you, and then on the trailer, suffering from frostbite, I have thought of nothing else.'

'I'm the same about you Alex.' I feel the heat rising in my cheeks.

We walk back hand in hand through the tangled trees, savouring each precious moment together.

Zosia's Journal, August – September, 1941
'An Unexpected Gift'
Two days after my walk in the forest with Alex, the strangest thing happened.

All morning was spent lumberjacking. I was walking back with the deportees along the water's edge to roll the next stack of timber to transport on the river. I was exhausted, physically and emotionally by the challenge of the unpredictable river.

As we walked back upstream, the soldiers were standing in a group, smoking and laughing at each other's jokes. Seeing them aroused pity in me; I felt sorry for them, for almost all of them, not for the two who had tried to assault me in the forest. I hadn't seen them again, thankfully, but for the rest of them. They were after all, just young men, some poor mothers' sons, who, like us, had been forced to be in this inhospitable place.

A young soldier was running towards the group, waving his arms and shouting.

'News! I have news from our Leader! And important orders!' He was very animated and was speaking excitedly. We could neither understand, nor hear every word, but it had to be something extremely important, as there was a lot of commotion and discussion amongst the young soldiers.

Eventually, the soldier in charge blew his whistle and ordered us all to line up. That was unheard of, we had never been told to stop working. We were supposed to float more logs down river to fulfil our quotas. What could be so important? He said that he had an announcement to make. The words that followed were the most unexpected he could have said.

'Go, you are free to leave.'

'What? Leave? where exactly? the forest, the camp, this place? What did he mean?' My heart was racing. A tiny part of me thought that he meant we could leave the camp. But that couldn't be right. That wasn't possible. We had all longed for some miracle to happen but we never really believed it would.

Some of the deportees asked him to explain what he meant, and what they had to do.

'Stop your work. Go back to the barracks now. Walk back. Don't wait for the carts and trailers. Pack your things, then leave the camp. You are free to go.'

The words echoed in my head over and over as I took them in. 'Pack your things… leave the camp…You are free to go.'

Part 4

Transit

Chapter 1

September – October 1941

'You are free to go.' Words Zosia had only dreamed of, the miracle they had prayed for in the unending night.

'*Our Father who art in Heaven.*' God was watching over them and had heard their prayers. But Alex? What about Alex?

Everyone who can, is running back to the barracks. Those who can't are hobbling or walking quickly and being helped by others. Zosia is being pulled along by the rush of frantic deportees. There is confusion on their faces and scenes of chaos as hundreds of deportees are desperately hurrying to leave. Zosia can't quite believe that they are being released. She should be euphoric. But her mind is a seesaw of conflicting choices: Alex or freedom, love or home. What is she going to do now?

There are hundreds of deportees from different work bases, all running and shouting. One of them, Henryk, who is fluent in Russian, is standing on an empty crate.

'Listen everyone! Listen!' he is shouting. The crowds quieten down. 'I overheard the soldiers talking. It is true. We are being released. Hurry, leave immediately, before there is any change of plan.'

Some of the deportees look delirious, others bewildered. The pace quickens to get back to barracks and leave.

Zosia wonders why this is happening. What could have happened to change everything so abruptly? But no one is stopping to ask. Zosia hears the deportees saying to each other:

'Just grab freedom with both hands and go.'

'We don't need explanations.'

'Thank God,' a deportee says, looking up to the heavens. Many of them are making the sign of the cross and saying prayers.

At the base camp, groups of deportees are already leaving, walking towards the iron gate, carrying the few tattered belongings they have, small bundles of clothes, rags, whatever they have managed to salvage, maybe a morsel of precious bread they have saved from their last rations. The majority carry nothing. Zosia hears them saying to each other:

'Emptyhanded we arrived, and emptyhanded we will leave.'

'I don't want anything that will remind me of this place.'

'I want nothing, except the greatest gift of all: freedom.'

Zosia is in sight of her barrack. Juzia, Lucia and Antoni are running to meet her. They are waving. Their smiling faces look happier than she has seen for a long time.

'Aunty Zosia, Mama and Papa said we are free. We are leaving the Camp,' says Lucia.

'Yes,' says Zosia and hugs the three of them.

'We are going home,' says Juzia.

Zosia walks towards the barrack. The girls are skipping and running ahead of her. Genia is approaching.

'Can you believe it Zosia? My God, this is what we've been hoping for,' says Genia. 'But we never thought it would really happen.'

'Yes,' Zosia says, twisting the ends of her scarf into a tight knot.

'We can go back home,' says Lucia. 'Will Rex be there?'

'I don't know,' says Zosia.

Lucia and Juzia are jumping up and down and dancing around. Antoni joins in.

'We're going on the sledge Father's made,' says Juzia.

'They're so excited,' says Genia. 'Hurry up Zosia, get your things from the barrack. We're leaving in a few minutes.' They start walking towards Wojtek who is carrying the sledge. But the question in Zosia's head won't be shut out: *Alex, where are you?*

It must be late September or maybe even early October. Juzef's 'glorious summer' is definitely over. The cold chill of the fast-approaching winter is already drifting in. It does not seem to matter as much now that they are leaving. The thought of another Siberian winter is not something they were looking forward to. Zosia's *sapogi* are wearing through again; she put fresh pieces of old newspaper into them that morning to keep the first, thin layers of snowfall from reaching her feet.

She starts walking to the barracks, thinking about Alex. 'When will I see him? I have to see him. Where is he? What am I going to do? I can't leave.'

A moment later, Genia calls out.

'Zosia, come on. We're leaving now.' She catches sight of her sister lifting Antoni and sees all three children sitting on the small sledge that Wojtek has made. They are ready to go.

'Genia, I can't…' she says. Genia turns around and sees Zosia.

'There you are. Come on, get on the sledge!' But Zosia can see there is no room for her, even if she had wanted to go with them. Genia and Wojtek are pulling it along. She would make it far too heavy, even if there had been enough space. Besides, she wouldn't be sitting on it, she would be helping to pull it. Zosia runs back to her sister.

'You go on ahead. Get yourselves and the children to the station; I'll catch you up. I'll see you there. I have to get my shawl. Don't worry about me.' They hug each other and Zosia kisses and hugs her young nieces and nephew.

Genia and Zosia are crying. 'Save yourself, save yourself, we love you, Zosia,' says Genia.

'There are two sleighs near the gates, filling up with deportees. Be sure to get on one of them, Zosia. We'll see you at the train station.'

'Yes, at the train station,' says Zosia. 'But don't wait for me if I'm not there. Get on the first train you can. Don't forget, I love you all.'

'We love you, Aunty Zosia.' The children's last words echo. They leave, waving at her, their parents pulling the sledge through the first snow out of the Labour Camp. When will she see them again?

And when will she see Alex? Will she see him? She has to see him.

She walks back towards the barracks to get her shawl.

'Zosia,' it is Alex's voice. She spins round.

'Alex, have you heard?'

'Yes.' His expression changes. He looks serious.

'Leave this place and come with me,' she says.

'I can't, they will kill my father if I leave.'

'Juzef can come too.'

'He will never leave. He knows nowhere else. Besides, we would never be able to get across the borders. They would never believe that we weren't Russian. But you, my darling Zosia, you must go, even though it breaks my heart.'

His eyes are full of tears but he smiles through them. He kisses her tenderly on the lips and she can feel one of his tears left on her cheek.

She touches the tear and kisses her finger. Her own tears start falling down her face.

'No, I can't go. I'll stay here with you. I don't want to leave you.'

'My darling Zosia, you can't do that. The soldiers will kill you, and me and father if they ever find out about us. You must leave. It's the only way to save yourself. When all this is over, this awful war, I promise I will come and find you. I will come to Poland, to Bortków and find you.'

They are both crying. They embrace, hug each other tightly and kiss. Wrapped in his arms, she is safe, secure. If only they could stay locked together in that moment, inseparable, like in a photograph, hugging each other forever.

'Remember, whatever happens, remember, I love you, always, Zosia.'

'I love you Alex,' she says through more tears. 'We don't have to part.'

'It's the only way we can survive. Take my heart with you,' he says.

'You already have mine,' she says.

They hug each other again and kiss again. The last kiss.

'I will find you. I promise, I will,' he says.

Tears are rolling down his face. Hers, unstoppable too. She watches him walk away, as in a dream, through the forest until she can no longer see him waving through the thick blackness of the trees. There is a huge lump in her throat and a stabbing ache deep inside her. Her heart is breaking.

Inside the hollow barrack, she falls on the bed and stares up at the bare ceiling. The familiar mustiness fills the cold space. She picks up her only possessions, the bag with her notebook and pen and her shawl, still damp, drying from the previous day. It is threadbare and ragged. She throws it over her shoulders.

For the last time, she looks round the place that has been their prison cell for the past year and a half. All trace of them is gone already. The only sign is the rusty nail protruding from the ceiling used to hang the saved rations on. The harsh blanket lies on the bed ready for the next poor 'enemies of the state.' She never wants to see the barrack again.

She walks out and pulls the door firmly shut behind her. Taking a deep breath, she lifts her eyes to the sky: '*Our Father who art in heaven,*' thank you for saving us. Please look after Alex and Juzef. Let Alex come and find me. Take care of Genia, Wojtek and the children. Keep them all safe. '*Thy Kingdom come, Thy will be done, on earth as it is in Heaven.*'

There is no sign of the two sleighs. They must have filled up quickly and gone. Droves of adults and children are heading towards the exit from the Labour Camp, like sheep funnelling through its gates. They are leaving on foot. Zosia joins them. She walks through the iron gates. There are no soldiers at the gates. No one is counting them. The barbed wire on top no longer imprisons them. Freedom. But, she leaves a part of herself there, with Alex. She clings on to his words:

'Whatever happens remember, I love you, always.'

'I promise I will come and find you.'

Bitter sweet tears of love and hope flow as she walks out through the gates.

'Take my heart,' he said. She leaves hers behind.

Chapter 2

It is late afternoon. The deportees are rushing to get as far away as possible from the camp in case the Russians change their minds. But where are they going? They are moving south and west, in the direction of home. Their guide is the disinclined sun, about to disappear below the horizon. Sunrise and sunset their compass points. On the journey to Siberia, the sun rose in front of them. Now it has to be behind them in the morning and light up the way in front of them as it sets.

The group Zosia is in walk for what is left of the day, without food or water, just what they may have left of their rations. They are starving, but they are used to this. The unexpected release is helping to overcome the hunger and block out the cold and discomfort a little. When nightfall comes, they fall asleep exhausted, finding shelter under the thick cloak of the forest.

The next morning, they wake from the cold and set off early. After several hours of walking, the edge of the forest is reached. They emerge from the pine trees, into the fields stretching out into the distance, as far as the eye can see. There are potatoes growing in the field. Their bellies are rumbling. They do what they did before, clawing them out of the soil with their bare hands. There is no cooking pot, no pan and no fire. They bite into the hard, soiled offerings, spewed up by this unforgiving host, and eat the raw potatoes, just as they did before on their journey to the Siberian camps.

How they would relish a bowl of 'szczy' soup now, or a morsel of bread.

They walk for days, covering miles, but progress is slow because many are sick and weak. They get better at surviving in the wild and feeding themselves. They make fires from wood they collect from the edge of the forests and cook food over an open fire. They collect nettles and any leaves they can find, and mix them with handfuls of snow to make soup. It is better than the zupa szczy they agree. They bake potatoes in the fire. The hot food and sitting round the open fire at night lifts their spirits further. They sing hymns in thanksgiving and songs from home. But the future is far from certain. Unknown and uncertain.

When the singing stops, the silence of sleep descends. Thoughts drift into Zosia's mind. She remembers the pain of separation. Alex's words, 'I'll come and find you,' remind her of her own to Helena.

'Where's Babcia Helena?' the children kept asking when they first arrived at the labour camp. They all missed their newly adopted grandmother. With all the best intentions in the world, they searched for Helena every day, in the food queues, on the trailers, in the forest. Zosia tried to think what work Helena could be doing and searched in the medical centre, and in the food store but she had not been able to find her anywhere.

'If only she had not been separated from us when we arrived at Noszul. If only I had said: 'She's our Babcia', to the soldiers, we would never have lost her.'

Then there was Genia's optimism on the train, about their brothers, on the first day of the deportation.

'They're just going to be in different wagons further up and down the train. We'll be able to see them when we stop.' Genia's words had provided reassurance as the train pulled out of the station for the first time. The thought that Adam would come and find them was comforting. She wanted to believe it, but it never happened. They should have protested but Adam knew it would make no difference. She lives in hope that one day she will see her brother.

The terrible pain at an early age caused by the most permanent separations, the deaths of her beloved mother and father. Separations completely beyond her comprehension at the time, and beyond her control.

But she knows that 'wanting' and 'hoping' something will happen is rarely enough, it is useless. She doesn't seem to have any control over what happens in her life. And now, Alex. The separation is unbearable. Will he ever find her? She has to believe he will. She has to live in hope. What else is there?

It is another bitter morning. Perhaps they will reach the station today. They walk for several hours. There is a thick mist on the plain in front of them. A ghostly mirage wavers in the distance. It looks like a row of saplings or sticks in the ground, some kind of fence or boundary perhaps. The young trees are swaying from side to side in the wind. Foliage on the saplings is fluttering. They seem to be moving closer. As they get nearer, Zosia realises that they are not young trees, nor sticks. What looked like foliage, is tattered rags. To her horror, the elongated shapes of human heads on the bodies of walking skeletons emerge from the fog like spirits rising from beyond the grave.

'Hello friends,' one of them says. 'Where are you going?' He speaks in Polish.

'Hello,' a deportee called Stanisław says. 'We are heading home. What about you?'

'We are POWs, Prisoners of War from the Gulags. We have been released and we are going back to our homes in Poland.'

They look like the walking dead: ashen-faced, shrunken, prematurely aged. Most are barefoot; others have rags and newspaper tied round their feet.[1]

'You look shocked,' the POW says.

'Forgive me, but you look so thin. If only we had some food to give you,' says Stanisław.

'Thin? Whatever do you mean? We are the best of the bunch from our Gulag,' he laughs. 'We are the strongest, the fittest. The rest of them, and there are many more, have been left behind. They can't move, let alone walk. They lie on the ground in rows hoping someone will take pity on them and bury them soon.'

Tears are rolling down the faces of the deportees listening.

Stanisław takes off his coat and gives it to the POW. Other deportees follow his example until every one of the POWs has a coat. 'What's your name?'

'I'm Paweł,' says the POW.

'Come with us Paweł. We will get some food, it may just be potatoes, and cook them for you.'

'Potatoes sounds wonderful,' says Paweł.

'What do you know about why we are all being released?' says Stanisław.

'All we know is that there is an Amnesty, and we're free,' says Paweł.

Later that evening, the deportees and the POWs are all warming themselves round a fire. The deportees cook what they can find and give most of it to the POWs. Zosia is nearby, she hears their conversation.

'Where is the Gulag you were in?' says Stan.

'I don't know exactly. Somewhere in the Arctic Circle. No one lives there, just us and the Polar Bears,' says Paweł.

'It was a terrible place,' says another POW, Janusz. 'We had to work in the lead mines. Of course, they're poisonous, most of our people died in them. We are the lucky ones.'

'The Russians are looking for gold,' says Pawel. 'They sent us to dig for it. But we didn't find any.'

'What about the Amnesty?' says Stan. Zosia listens. She is not sure what it means exactly.

'It is a strange word to use for our circumstances,' says the deportee, Henryk. 'An 'amnesty' is a pardon, for a crime or an offence. But we haven't committed any crime, unless you count living in eastern Poland.'

'Yes, that's it. That's the offence they're forgiving you for. That made you 'enemies of the state',' says Paweł. 'But us, our crime was that we were in the Polish army. They took our weapons away and sent us to the Gulags for that.

'Or we spoke up for democracy in Poland, or had an uncle or cousin who did,' says Janusz.

Stan stokes the fire with a stick. After a while, he says:

'We don't know any more than you about the Amnesty. The plan is to get to the nearest railway station, Noszul we think, and get on a train heading south and back home.'

Chapter 3

Six or seven days after leaving the camp, what looks like a farmstead and a village come into view. There are a number of farm buildings. Further along there is a path and a row of small houses. There are people on the path and more are working in the fields surrounding the farm.

'We need to take care. It might be dangerous,' says Stan. 'Wait here everyone, I'll go and speak to them. Henryk, please come with me, we'll probably need to speak in Russian.'

When they return, it turns out to be quite the opposite of dangerous. The villagers are bringing out food and drink for everyone. They too seem shocked by the appearance of the POWs and also of the deportees.

'We don't realize how bad we look,' says Zosia to Eva, a young girl, about the same age as her in the group.

'But I can see it in their eyes.'

'No, we haven't washed for a long time, and I'm skinnier than I've ever been,' says Eva.

'Me too. When we get home, we can eat as many doughnuts and '*pierogi*' (dumplings) as we want,' says Zosia.

Eva's pale complexion and sunken cheeks make her look frail. Her hair is matted and tangled.

No one in the group looks well. How could they? But their appearance is the least of their worries.

The villagers bring freshly baked bread with ham, cheese and honey and hot chai. It was like manna from heaven. They give them hot beetroot and potato soup, all of which provides some long-needed nourishment. The kindness and generosity of these poor villagers, who must be living hard lives in these remote surroundings, is touching.

'Where are you from?' asks one of the women ladling out the soup.

'From Poland. We are going back there,' says Eva.

'It's a long way. Have you heard about the Amnesty and what the Polish Army is doing?'

'The Amnesty, yes. But not about the Polish Army,' says Zosia.

The woman pulls out a newspaper from her basket and shows it to them.

'Look at this,' she says, pointing at pictures of the man called Hitler and German soldiers driving tanks. Zosia remembers the name from the cartoon she had seen. In Russian and some broken Polish, she tells Zosia and Eva what the headline says.

'Betrayal, Traitors.' The Germans have betrayed our

country. They have invaded more of Poland and now they have invaded Russia. They were our allies. But now they are shooting our soldiers and our people, and driving their tanks over our land.'

'What about the Polish Army?' says Zosia.

'Come with me,' says the woman.

On the wall of one of the houses, she shows her and Eva a poster. There is the same picture of Stalin she had seen before on it. Stan, Henryk and others are already there looking at it. Henryk is translating it.

'Russia and Poland, allies against the common enemy, Germany.

The Russian state authority gives permission to the Polish Army to form in Russia to help in the fight against Germany.

All Russian citizens must assist the Polish people and direct them to join their army base in Buzułuk.'

The name of the place stands out in big letters.

'Where is that?' Stan asks.

'We don't know exactly. The best thing is to go to Noszul, the nearest railway station. They will direct you from there,' says the villager.

'How far is Noszul from here?'

'Not far, about fifteen miles. Head due south.'

The villagers offer to transport the weaker members of the group in their farm carts and wagons. The mothers with young children and the POWs go.

They thank the villagers for their generosity and kindness. Most of all, the deportees are grateful for the news of a Polish Army base within their reach. Now they have a clear goal. They set off on the last leg to the station.

At the station Zosia is looking around for Genia, Wojtek and the children among the crowds and for anyone she recognises from the camp who could have seen them. Her sister and family and those on the sleighs must have left the station days ago. It has taken her more than a week to reach Noszul on foot. There are crowds of unfamiliar faces from different labour camps and gulags. They hear from snatches of conversation that the numbers of deportees fleeing across the country from north to south are immense. Thousands more are escaping from camps in Kazakhstan. They are given full rations from that point on, as they are now an ally of Russia, on the main route to the Polish Military headquarters.

'Feeding and moving the tsunami of people flooding southwards across the country to Buzułuk is a huge task,' says Henryk.

'How many are there?' says Stan.

'I don't know. It must be around a million, maybe two million people on the move to Buzułuk,' says Henryk.

From Noszul the train takes them south. A couple of hours later, they have to change trains and the guards tell them they need to get to a station, twenty miles away, to continue south.

After another night, followed by another three day's walking, they arrive near the station the guards told them about.

As they come over the hill, Zosia can see a small town sprawling up the sides of a green valley. They are heading further and further south, Zosia begins to feel the tepid warmth of the sun increasing. In amidst the houses and trees, she catches sight of the glimmer of metal from a train. There must be about a hundred deportees and POWs in the group. How will they all get on the train? None of them have any money, they have nothing at all to offer in payment of a fare. It seems an impossible situation. But undeterred, and in a state someway between blind determination and delirium, they are going to try their hardest. Stan, Henryk and a few others go on ahead to the station to negotiate.

The majority of the group wait on the hill, sharing some of their thoughts with one another.

'What would have happened to us if this turnaround had not occurred?'

'Who knows? We would probably have remained in Siberia for the rest of our lives and perished there.'

'We have lost so many of our fellow countrymen and women in the Soviet Union and on the journey here.'

'But we mustn't give up. We just need to get to the Polish Army base. We need to focus on that. We're nearly there.'

'We are on the way out of this nightmare: we're going home at last.'

Three hours pass when the group returns. What they said to the station master, no one knows, but he agreed to take all the deportees as far towards their destination as the train can take them. Zosia and Eva are overjoyed at the news and thankful to have Stan and Henryk taking care of them. They stay on the hill overnight and make their way down to the station in the morning.

What they do not realise until they get to the station, is that it is awash with deportees and POWs all trying to do the same thing. There are huge numbers on the platform, not visible from their hilltop refuge. Thousands of semi-starved, emaciated survivors are hanging on to life by the thinnest of threads and many of them not making it any further, but dying on the platform.

Train after train leaves packed with the escaping hopefuls. It is heart-breaking to see families being separated; children and even a baby, are pushed onto the train by parents in a desperate attempt to at least save their offspring if not themselves, at whatever cost. Many of the trains do not even stop at the station as they are already completely full.

Zosia and her friends go into the fields in search of food. They are harvesting the usual potatoes and beetroot. At that moment, one of their group, Marek, comes running up and shouting:

'Quick, an empty train is coming, and we are supposed to be on it!'

They are about half a mile from the station. They start running.

'Come on Zosia,' says Eva.

'I can't go any faster. You go on ahead,' says Zosia. She is not able to run as fast as the others, due to the injury to her leg. Although it has recovered from the break, she has a limp. With no other option, she hobbles as fast as she can. By now the train is ready to leave, steam is belching out of its chimney. The group must all be on board, just a few stragglers left. Then the train starts to move. Zosia panics, she cannot bear the thought of being left behind. A few of the boys jump off to help the stragglers. Zosia is running as fast as she can. The train is fully in sight. As she runs down the final slope to the railway track, she trips on the uneven ground. As she trips, there is a loud click, followed by a strange sensation in her leg. Her leg feels better. She is no longer limping. She can run normally. The trip succeeds in clicking it back into its rightful place. She speeds up. As she gets close to the train, she sees Eva and catches hold of her outstretched hand. She jumps on to the train along with the others. No one is left behind this time. With a broad grin on her face, she walks up and down in the carriage. Her limp has disappeared. The break has miraculously righted itself and she can walk without limping.

'Oh Alex, if only you could see me now. If only you could be here with me and share my joy. You saw me when I had broken my leg and when I had frostbite, when I was at my worst, and bedraggled, but you loved me anyway. How I miss you. I love you Alex.'

Chapter 4

Zosia's Journal – Buzułuk 1941

We're on the train now to Buzułuk. Finally, we are on the last leg of the journey to the Polish Army Base and from today, we are a huge step closer to getting back home. Henryk told us that the distance from Noszul to Buzułuk was about 725 miles as the crow flies. It took us over a week to reach Noszul on foot from the Labour Camp. We have had to change trains a number of times as there is no direct line between Noszul and Buzułuk. But we are nearly there.

The journey is long and uncomfortable, in more dreary cattle wagons. They are no longer shocking. Everything is more bearable because there is one important difference from the first time on the train – we are free. Many of the passengers are smiling and sharing their relief. They talk about their homes in Poland.

'We're going home,' can be heard throughout the wagon.

'Don't count your chickens,' some others say.

It is getting warmer each day as we move further south. That is helping too, having a positive effect on everyone. For so long we have been deprived of the sun's heat. Now the wagon doors are left unlocked. We can open and shut them when we want. We have light, we can breathe fresh air and look out at far-reaching views.

Eva and I make new friends in the wagon with two girls about our age, Sabina and Hanka from one of the other labour camps. We stand at the edge of the wagon, with the doors open, stick our heads out and shriek with joy as the warm breeze hits our faces.

The train guards are no longer hostile. We get rations, although they continue to be low. But for some of the released POWs and deportees it is too late. They are dying on the train from starvation and disease caused by poor hygiene. Corpses are left by the side of the tracks. The death of these victims, so near to the end of our ordeal, is perhaps even more tragic than that of the deportees who died on the journey into Siberia. These were not spared the horrors of the Prisoner of War and Labour Camps.

After over a week on the train, we catch sight of something in the distance. In the heat haze of the desert landscape, we spot the movement from left to right and from right to left of a tiny red dot. We don't know what it is. It disappears from view. As we get nearer, we are able to make out the shape of row upon row of pale khaki-coloured tents, camouflaged against the mounds of yellowy-brown desert sand, merging with them in the shimmer of the haze.

Excitement at the prospect that we have reached Buzułuk is rising. Without doubt, it is a military encampment of some kind. It has to be the Polish army base. We round a bend. The sight of the red and white of a Polish flag fluttering above one of the tents comes into full view and confirms our hopes. The 'red' of the flag is the distant 'dot', the first thing we saw from far away and were unable to identify. Shouts of 'We've made it,' 'We're coming home,' and cheering break out. Singing of the national anthem starts nearby and spreads throughout the length of the train. At long last, we have reached the goal of our journey of the past few months. This is Buzułuk. The gateway to home.

Many are in tears around me, like children returning to the unconditional love of their mother after suffering an unjustifiable ill. The release from captivity, the imminent protection under the wing of the Polish armed forces, none of this could have been foreseen. Here we are, our fate being spun out against the backdrop of an unthinkable situation. A unique situation, Polish troops assembling on Russian soil as allies with those who deported and enslaved us.

'*Forgive us our trespasses, as we forgive those who trespass against us.*'

It must be evening, the sun is just beginning to dip in the sky, signalling the welcome respite from the blazing heat of the day. The faint sounds around the tents reach our ears, the clink and rattle of crockery and cutlery and the low hum of conversation punctuated by occasional laughter. The smell of cooked food; a mixture of meat juices and vegetables floats towards us, activating our appetites, even more than usual. As we get nearer, we peer out from behind the tents. We can see the clearing up of the dinner plates taking place and lines of soldiers sitting on benches at wooden tables. The Polish Army. A sorry sight. A collection of emaciated humanity in baggy, oversized uniforms They are the released POWs and Labour Camp deportees and bear all the signs of their undeserved suffering.

Some are getting up and moving away, a few sharing a cigarette, drawing in with what looks like great pleasure before passing it on to another wretch next to them. Others sit chatting and laughing at the tables, while some are collecting plates and dishes and taking them to the open-air kitchens to be washed. The majority are men.

At tables on the right there are women, dressed in the same oversized uniforms and equally wretched. Amongst them is a tall, thin woman who stands out from the rest. She appears to be in charge. From the front, she is addressing the group. They are all listening. She must be giving them important information or orders. She finishes speaking, glances at her watch and dismisses them. A similar process is taking place at the men's tables.

We split up into smaller groups and approach cautiously. This is the moment we have all been waiting for: the longed-for acceptance into the army, the essential step in pursuit of the dream of returning home, and our freedom. But it is not as I imagined. There is no running into the open arms of the Commanding Officer or falling to the ground with gratitude. Quite the opposite, embarrassed and ashamed of our wretched and dirty appearance, we are uncertain about what to do. We decide to watch and listen behind one of the tents until it feels safe to come out.

Once all the soldiers are dismissed, the woman in charge sits down and begins writing. After some time, a small group of us, girls and women, who have become separated from the main group, decide this could be a good time to emerge. Tentatively, we walk towards her, self-conscious of our ragged clothes and aware of the scratching noise of our tattered shoes on the gritty ground. Alerted by this curious sound, she looks up, turns around and sees us.

She has the most piercing hazel eyes. Beneath these jewelled, amber-like spheres is a freckled face and a rather large mouth. She is uniquely attractive. Her first look at us is grave and almost frightening, but then the large mouth spreads into a wide smile and the warm eyes beam with kindness.

'And where have you come from my dear women?' she says.

It's the first time anyone has ever called me 'woman'. We are dirty, our faces grey and wrinkled from the dry heat, our hair matted, we must look older than we really are. Hanka is only 16, Sabina is 17, the same age as me, and Eva is 18. I suppose we are women, or very nearly. There are some women who are much older, maybe 40 or 50 years old.

'From Siberia,' we say, and tell her that we don't know the exact name of the places where we have been. The answer seems to satisfy her. She looks round at each of us in the group. Perhaps recognising that some of us are young, she says,

'My dear girls,' Her eyes fill and brim with tears, 'You have travelled a long way. Welcome to Buzułuk. Welcome. I am Commandant Bronisława and I will be in charge of you.

She asks us when we last had a proper, cooked meal. None of us can remember exactly. She must be aware of the conditions we have been under. She summons a meal for us immediately. And what a meal it is. Our first taste of hot, cooked food since we left Poland except for what the villagers gave us a few weeks back. A stew of meat and vegetables, neither of which, apart from uncooked potatoes, beetroot and cabbage, have we seen or tasted for over a year and a half. We fill our bellies. But we cannot eat all of it. Our stomachs have shrunk so much because of the limited rations we have been on. A feast has been placed before us, but most of us can only manage a part of it. Those who gorge themselves and eat more than their bodies can tolerate, are sick and in pain.

There is fruit for dessert. I will never forget the first bite of the first apple that day, a taste and texture denied us for so long. How impoverished we had become, that the humble apple could provide the most exquisite taste.

When we finish eating, the Commandant returns. She tells us that we should get some sleep. But before that, we need to get cleaned up. We are taken to the showers: wooden cubicles in the sand and buckets of water warmed up by the sun. What delight, we scrub and scrub to wash away the dirt of months. We are de-loused. We use paraffin on our hair to rid it of nits and fleas and when we comb it, an effort in itself, as we have had no brush or comb for all the time we have been travelling, a variety of wildlife escapes the tangled mass and is washed away and returned to the ground. Our clothes: the tattered, flea-infested rags, are taken away to be burned. They are replaced by clean army uniforms. We are each given two sets of new underwear and a nightdress. We are taken to tents with rows of camp beds. Sabina, Eva, Hanka and I get four bunks together. That night and for much of the next day, the four of us sleep like babies. We are exhausted by the long struggle to survive and the hundreds of miles we have travelled to get here.

Waking up on the morning of the following day, I feel refreshed, reborn. For the first time since leaving home, I wake up warm. My thoughts turn to Genia and the children. I set out to look for them. There are hundreds of tents full of civilians and families in the camp. I scour the area for my sister and Juzia, Lucia and Antoni, following the long-unheard sound of children's voices laughing and playing, hoping to find my nieces and nephew among them. But I do not find them. I resolve to try again the next day and every day until I succeed.

This newfound existence of comparative milk and honey continues for a time. The Commandant looks after us, she takes good care of us. In return we do whatever work is needed: cleaning, helping in the kitchens or assisting the few medical staff that there are in the first aid tent.

More and more POWs and deportees pour into the camp every day. It quickly becomes clear that the rations the Soviet Union is supplying are far from sufficient. The soldiers are making do on half rations so that everyone can at least have something to eat. We all do the same. There is no punishment here for sharing food with one another.

'*Give us this day our daily bread.*'

The Polish Commander-in-Chief, General Władysław Sikorski, Prime Minister of Poland, is due at the base.

We line up outside at eight o'clock in the morning ready for his arrival. He inspects the ranks. During his brief visit, he speaks to all assembled. He praises us for our endurance of the intolerable situation we have been in, and encourages us not to give up. We should thank God for looking after us. The worst is behind us and we are now on our way back home. He tells us that he is returning to London where the Polish Government in Exile is now based.

This is followed a week or two later by a visit from the Commander of the Polish Army in the Soviet Union, General, Władysław Anders. We are briefed by our superiors about General Anders before his visit. For the past two years, he has been imprisoned in Lubyanka jail in Moscow, one of the harshest Soviet jails. We have him to thank for our present situation. He has been instrumental in the negotiations for the release of all detainees and in discussions with Stalin over the formation of the Polish Army in the Soviet Union. His military headquarters are in the town of Buzułuk, in a building provided by the Soviets.

We do not need to line up when he comes. We should just go about our daily work or whatever we are doing. He wants to see how the camp is working and assess supplies.

Conditions have deteriorated as more fall ill and the camp begins to look more and more like a refugee camp full of the sick and hungry, which after all, is what it is, and not a shipshape army camp. My friends and I spend more and more time working in the mushrooming medical tents, looking after those suffering from dysentery and other diseases.

On the day of the General's visit, we are in one of the hospital tents, helping the few doctors to take care of the sick. General Anders visits the hospital tents. He speaks to the sick and dying soldiers and civilians. He does not leave any of them out in our tent. Then he speaks to the doctor.

'What do you need? Do you have enough medicines? Just make a list of anything you need and send it to me. I will make sure you get it,' he says.

The doctor thanks him and tells him about the limited food supplies which are causing some of the problems because most people are existing on half rations, so everyone can have something to eat.

'Leave it with me. I will do whatever I can,' he says.

Sabina, Hanka, Eva and I are tending to the sick. He turns to us, smiles and says,

'You are angels, you are doing wonderful work, God bless you all.'

He leaves the tent talking to the senior officer accompanying him.

* * *

Two days after General Anders's visit, there is a briefing from Commandant Bronisława. She asks the women what they know about the Amnesty and events that led up to it. All any of them know is that Germany invaded Russia and that somehow caused the Amnesty, but they do not know any more than that.

'That's right,' says the Commandant. 'Germany attacked Russia, who was its ally up to that point. It started on the 22nd June 1941, in what is known as, 'Operation Barbarossa.' The Germans took over most of Poland and were attacking the Russian troops in Białystock, Lwów and other Polish cities, as well as at airports on the eastern side of Poland being used by the Russian military. On the 30th June, they invaded the Soviet Union, attacking Leningrad, the Ukraine and Moscow. But they failed to capture Moscow.

The Soviet Union, sought to defend itself from the German hostilities, by joining the Allied forces. This included France, Britain and others, who had previously been their enemy, against the now common opposing force. Poland and Russia were now on the same side in the war against Germany.

For all of us detained in Russia, this was the most incredibly lucky stroke of fate. For all the deportees and POWs imprisoned in the depths of Siberia, Kazakhstan and other parts of the Soviet Union, it was a miracle. As a result of the turnaround of events, General Anders, one of the few, incidentally who had predicted the German treachery, was released from wrongful imprisonment in Moscow. He took the opportunity, offered by Stalin, to join forces, realising that the creation of a military presence was critical to freeing and removing all detainees from the Soviet Union. The Polish Prime Minister, General Sikorski together with Anders negotiated the release of all prisoners. A Polish-Soviet agreement was signed, the Sikorski-Maisky Pact on 30th July, 1941. All Polish detainees were to be released under the terms of an 'Amnesty.' The process of release from the labour camps started after the official declaration was made on 12th August and it is still going on. That's why more and more deportees are still arriving every day.

In order that we could become useful allies in the fight against Germany, the agreement allowed for the formation of a Polish army on Russian territory. This would have been out of the question in normal circumstances. Nothing like this had ever happened before. But the Russian authorities needed to strengthen their defences on all fronts. They would be able to deploy the Polish forces wherever needed. This could well be in the Middle Eastern oilfields of Iraq, Kurdistan and Turkmenistan, which are currently under threat of German invasion.

We are being supplied with rations by the Soviet Union as they are responsible for the forced deportation and imprisonment of all those detained in the Soviet Union. Estimates of the numbers vary and there are thousands of civilians, including children to feed. Stalin has agreed to supply rations for 30,000 troops. But the numbers are greater and still growing fast. The Polish and Soviet ideas about the size of the army are very different. General Anders wants to get all the detainees, including all civilians out of Russia. He is negotiating for the immediate supply of increased rations. Any questions?' Commandant Bronisława ends. There are none.

Zosia and her friends walk back to the medical tents.

'It's all beginning to make more sense now, from these fragments of information,' says Sabina.

'Like pieces of a jigsaw,' says Zosia.

'But it seems so random, as if someone is throwing a dice to decide what happens. One minute we're prisoners, the next we're free,' says Eva.

'We are lucky to be alive and free,' says Hanka.

'Someone must be watching over us,' says Sabina.

'God heard our prayers,' says Eva. 'He is leading us out of the land of captivity. But how on earth are we going to get safely back home?

'*Deliver us from evil.*'

January 1942

News is spreading through the camp that the army may be moving any day, unless the food supplies are increased. We are told to get ready and make sure our papers are in order and show that we are signed up to the army.

But despite all the care and acceptance which we have experienced at the army base, there is one major stumbling block that some of us still have to overcome. To officially join the army, we have to be eighteen. Quite a few of us, including Sabina, Hanka and me, are too young. Only

Eva is eighteen. To join the army, we have to fulfil certain criteria. Firstly, to have been a Polish resident citizen in Poland before the first of September 1939. Secondly, we must have been born between 1897 and 1923. We are too young by a year, and Hanka, by two. There are quite a few girls in the same boat. All this time, we have been housed, fed, trained and employed. The authorities have protected us. Where else can we go? Who else will be our guardians and protectors in this war? Now the military situation is about to change, our futures are at stake. There are rumours that women and children are going to be sent to India and Africa. Out of humanitarian compassion, they have offered to take orphaned children and families.

But we do not belong to those categories. Besides, as single young women, we are desperate to be a part of the fight for Poland. The only way to achieve this is to stay with the Army. It is our best chance of survival and of getting to Europe and back to Poland.

The Commandant tells us that we are too young and therefore we will need to stay behind and wait for the civilian evacuation. She does not know yet when that will be, and we are terrified of this uncertainty and of the even worse possibility of being sent back to Siberia. After all, anything is possible. This provides us with more than sufficient incentive not to take any risks and do whatever is necessary to follow the far safer option of keeping with the army, even though the army has clearly stated that it cannot take us with them. We have to come up with a plan.

The troops are preparing to leave Buzułuk camp. The three of us agonise over what we need to do. On the morning the army is due to depart, we pull out our beds from the side of the tent, climb underneath and hide inside the extremely narrow space between the bunks and the edge of the tent. As we are thin, it is easily achievable. When the Commandant comes in looking for us, we are invisible. We have to remain completely still and quiet, trying desperately not to give ourselves away by breathing loudly or sneezing, in order that the slightest sound does not expose us. Our bags are gone. We have put them with the other soldiers' bags on the trucks ready to go. As there is no sign of us, she will probably assume that we have already left.

It is only much later that day, when the troops are setting off in their convoy, that we emerge. We go to the Commandant, who doesn't seem too surprised by our presence. We plead with her to be allowed to stay with the army.

'We are only slightly too young. We can't stay here alone. What would happen to us? We would die here and never get back home. We can be useful to the army in many ways and we are not afraid to join the fight. We are eager to do so.'

The civilian trucks heading for the villages have long since departed. Luckily, she seems to have a soft spot for us and sympathises with our situation.

'Right, get the paperwork done,' she says. 'Make sure your date of birth is correct on the forms. Remember, you must be eighteen to join the army. 1923 is the latest date of birth the army is accepting.'[1] We read between the lines. And so, we are creative about our date of birth and make ourselves slightly older, to achieve the goal of leaving the USSR under the wing of the Polish Army. My date of birth changes to 1st March 1923. Commandant Bronisława signs our papers and we love her.

Chapter 5

Zosia's Journal January 1942

Today we left Buzułuk, officially signed up members of the Polish Army, the II Corps, which had informally become known as, 'Anders's Army.' The transfer to Uzbekistan at the beginning of 1942 took almost a week by train from Totskoye to Tashkent, covering a distance of around 1,312 miles. It was even longer by road, as those making the journey in trucks testified.

The Commandant tells us that General Anders is based at the military headquarters in a place called, Yangi-Yul. The formation of the army into military divisions is beginning to take place and training for combat is due to start in the next few days. Unfortunately, she says, the divisions are dispersed over a very large area of Uzbekistan; in some cases, hundreds of miles from the headquarters. Some divisions are located in Kirghizstan, Kazakhstan and Tadzhikistan. I have never heard of any of these places and have no idea where any of them are. We are stationed in the depths of southern Uzbekistan, at a place called Guzar.

Training starts almost immediately, but most of the recruits are undernourished and weak. The excessive daytime heat, which is up to 35 degrees, means that it has to be done in the cooler parts of the day. We have come out of the land of extreme cold to one of extreme heat, out of the fridge into the fire. Mosquitoes thrive, resulting in widespread outbreaks of malaria, and other unknown diseases. My friends and I work in the hospital tents helping the sparse number of doctors and nurses.

March 1942

We were briefed today that the number of military personnel in the Polish Army has grown to approximately 70,000. This has by far exceeded Russian expectations for the provision of rations. General Anders and Stalin have again discussed extra rations for all members of the army. Stalin has agreed to increase supplies to 44,000, but only until the end of the month. There is no option left for the army but to start evacuating the surplus 30,000 troops. All the troops will be leaving the Soviet Union by the end of March. To avoid the cliff edge and due to the escalating numbers affected by disease and death, the troop evacuation is to start immediately. We are moving out tomorrow for Iran, previously known as Persia, where the army will come under the command of the British forces.

My friends and I, the under-age co-conspirators, board the army trucks for the first part of our journey out of the Soviet Union from Guzar to Tashkent. We cannot believe that at long last, we are leaving the Soviet Union. But as usual in the Soviet Union, everywhere is a huge distance away and everywhere takes a long time to reach. Added to this, nowhere ever seems to be on a direct route. The trucks take us as far as a railway station, where trains have been re-routed to provide us with passage for part of the journey. We then transfer to trucks across the desert and through the mountains to somewhere in Turkmenistan, a total journey of around 1,176 miles. I cannot remember how many days or weeks it took or all the exotic names, of still more unfamiliar places. Some still echo in my head: Samarkand, Tashkent.

After hours crossing the arid monotony of the desert, there are buildings, dwellings, some kind of town. I wipe the sand from my face and my eyelashes with the sleeve of my shirt and shake it from my hair. When I look up, the most welcome sight greets us. I remember it very well, because it is here that for the very first time in my life, I set eyes on the sea. It is the Caspian Sea, we are told. The sight of the lustrous, shifting expanse of sapphire lifts my spirits beyond imagination and the prospect of sailing across it offers not only the passage of the final release from the Soviet Union, but pure hope, taking us a very big step nearer to home and freedom.

When we arrive at the quayside and get out of the trucks, the Commandant addresses us. She tells us that we have arrived at Krasnovodsk, a huge oil port, serving the Baku oilfields in Azerbaijan, on the eastern shores of the Caspian Sea. It is full of all kinds of vessels from rusty, old industrial ships and oil tankers to fishing boats. We will be making the crossing from here to Iran. We wait on the quayside for further instructions.

It was only a little later that we discovered, any available vessel was being used to evacuate the troops, from the large tankers to the smallest fishing boats, and it could take anything between twenty-four hours and up to several days to make the sea crossing to Bandar-e-Pahlevi, also known as Bandar-e-Anzali in Iran.

The sea passage was difficult, conditions were extremely overcrowded. People were crammed onto the various boats. The weakest were dispatched first. The strongest were left till last, as they would be most likely to survive the longest. Eva, Sabina, Hanka and I made the crossing on one of the oil tankers. It was so full of people and the deck so close to the water, that we were terrified that the boat was in danger of sinking. Conditions were deplorable for everyone, especially for the sick who were lying on the deck with no shelter from the glaring sun. There was no food and very little water. The four toilets between around five to six hundred people were totally inadequate and very quickly, overflowing. More became sick with the spreading typhoid and dysentery, not to mention sea-sickness due to the large waves which were spilling onto the deck.

Commandant Bronisława despatched us to help the small medical team on board. My heart went out to the sick and starving soldiers. They were emaciated, their bodies riddled with wounds and sores. We did whatever we could to help them, using the limited water resources to hydrate them, trying to clean their sores, holding their hands and comforting them. We witnessed many deaths on the journey, and many unceremonious burials at sea. The corpses of those who died nearer the arrival port were taken off the boat and transported to the cemetery in Pahlevi for burial. I saw the trucks being loaded with the dead, some of whom I had looked after in their last hours on the boat. By the time we left, the Commandant later said that there was a total of 568 Polish graves in the cemetery in Pahlevi.

When we first set foot in Pahlevi, we were overcome with mixed emotions: ecstatic to be finally free from the land of our unjustified detention. But, at the same time, for those who had lost family members in the Soviet Union, there was further heartbreak, knowing that they were leaving their loved ones behind forever. Some had died much earlier during the deportation and had been left along the train tracks or buried in the Siberian forests. Others, who perished on the last leg of the journey were swiftly disposed of in the Caspian Sea. Many of the deportees were hobbling down the gangplank, fighting tears of unfathomable grief with those of joy and relief, and vowing never to return to the Soviet Union.

The local crews meeting the ship looked at us with eyes full of pity for the poor wretches before them, victims of the atrocities of the labour camps. But the deportees were smiling through their tears. Many were falling to their knees, kissing the ground of the liberating host country and hailing General Anders as their Moses for leading them out of the land of their enslavement.

The Iranian crews and local people welcomed us warmly, with open arms, and with great generosity, bringing hot, sweet tea, dates, fruit and pastries. The locals were clearly moved by what they were seeing. Polish, British and Indian officers met us. They too looked shocked by the state and appearance of the arriving 'army'. We were led to the beach area, where we were able to get cleaned up in the tents and showers prepared for our arrival. All the evacuees washed, were deloused, had a shave and a haircut. They received fresh, lightweight uniforms, suitable for the southern latitudes. Heaps of civilian clothes and shoes, much of which had been donated by the USA, were available for us on the white-sand, palm-fringed beaches of Pahlevi.

I later learned that between the 24th March and the 5th April 1942 over 30,000 soldiers and over 12,000 civilians succeeded in being evacuated across the Caspian Sea.[1] By the end of August, the last evacuation was completed. But there are still many deportees and POWs left in the Soviet Union. Plans are being made to move them to various British Colonies, among them Africa and India.

From Pahlevi we travel in trucks and lorries across the Elburz mountains to army camps in Tehran. We are in a humid, subtropical climate, once again in temperatures of 30 degrees Celsius, plus. Nothing can be a greater contrast to what we experienced in the Arctic conditions of Siberia.

The mountains are criss-crossed by treacherous, narrow roads, if they can be called 'roads', with sheer precipices on either side. It is an extremely bumpy and at times, a terrifying ride. I am in the back of a truck with the sick, tending to them and trying to protect them. I do what I can to keep them hydrated and wipe them with the fresh, cool water we have been given, which helps to keep their temperatures down.

From the back of the truck, beyond the flapping tarpaulin covers, the magnificent landscape and the precipitous road winding its way up the mountain side stretches out in all directions. The spectacular sight below is dangerously exciting. I admire and secretly envy the Iranian driver's challenge and wish that one day I will be able to learn to drive.

We stay in a camp near Tehran for around three months. But as that part of Iran is under Soviet control, and relations are becoming tenser, we move on to Qizil Rabat in Iraq, which is under British occupation, and join the training camps near Mosul and Kirkuk. The II Corps comes under the authority of the British Army, who provides us with food, supplies and uniforms.

We are stationed in a desert zone. Conditions are harsh. In the daytime it is unbearably hot, over 40 degrees Celsius, and at night temperatures fall to below freezing. Our hair turns yellow from the blazing sun and our skin burns. We fail to protect ourselves from the blistering heat, never having experienced temperatures like this. The girls and I continue working in the makeshift hospital in the desert camp. Training by fire. We soon pass the medical tests required to become qualified nurses.

Scorpions and lizards crawl in the tents, on the patients and their beds. Mosquitoes beset the camp and more troops are infected with malaria. The medical staff work hard in the hospital under extreme conditions. According to the doctors, during the six months until August 1942, 49,500 cases of diseases, predominantly typhoid and malaria, are treated by the Polish Army Hospitals. [2]

There are many sick and dying patients who need our help. One of them, I remember very well, was Andrzej, a boy of eighteen. He was so thin, he was just skin and bone, and suffering from typhoid. He always smiled when the nurses or doctors came to him, even though he was in great pain. We had run out of morphine. There was none left for him. He told me about his home town, Róvno, and about his family who had all been deported. His parents did not reach the labour camps, they both died on the journey out to Siberia. His younger brother, Zbyszek perished in the forests at the labour camp when a felled tree landed on him and killed him. His sister, Marysia, was the only survivor of the family, apart from himself. Although he did not know where she was, he was happy to think that she must still be alive. After he told me this, he smiled at me through his pain and asked for a drink of water. I went to get it for him. A moment later, when I returned, he had died; his eyes wide open staring up to heaven with his smile preserved. I couldn't help thinking what a terrible waste of a young man's life. He had not even been an adult at the beginning of the war, just an innocent teenager.

I hold the hands of many poor souls as they pass away in my arms over months. The situation is hopeless, we are unable to help them. There is little medication available. The minimal staff of doctors and nurses are ill-equipped to deal with the avalanche of disease. There is no 'spirytus' to deal with the wounds and suffering of the dying and to ease their pain. I cannot run and get it, as I did in vain to save my beloved, dying father.

'Papa, why is this happening? Papa, Mama, where are you? Jesus help us.'

The next year we train and spend time travelling in trucks across the Middle East, through Iraq, across the Syrian deserts, Lebanon and to Palestine. During the stay in Palestine, there is more training in readiness for combat, when we are not working as nurses.

One early morning, as Eva and I are walking to the Hospital tents, a group of soldiers are walking towards us. They are carrying rucksacks on their backs and look as if they are leaving the camp for manoeuvres. Among them I recognise Henryk from the labour camp.

'Hello,' he says. The group of soldiers moves ahead, but Henryk stops.

'I see you are nurses now. That's wonderful. We have all come such a long way from the camp.'

Eva asks him where he is off to. His reply surprises us.

'I'm glad I've seen you both because we will probably not see each other again. We are leaving the Army.' He tells us that General Anders has given Jewish members of the II Corps the option of remaining in Palestine. He has told them that, 'The choice of staying with the army and fighting Nazi Germany or remaining in Palestine and fighting for a Jewish state is up to the individual.'[3]

Henryk had made his choice. He was staying there.

'It is my homeland,' he said. 'I hope you get back to yours. Good luck to you both and God bless you.'

We shake hands with him and he gives us a big hug and a kiss.

'Good luck and God bless you too, Henryk,' I say.

He runs to catch up with the other soldiers walking out of the camp. Anders had indeed delivered them to the promised land. There was no doubt he would do the same for the rest of us.

It is December and we are in the Holy Land. Eva, Sabina, Hanka and I cannot believe it. When the Commandant tells us that there is a possibility of going to Bethlehem on Christmas Eve, we are speechless with delight.

'We may be able to visit the church in Bethlehem, but if not, it will be enough to see it from the outside and perhaps hear the singing,' she says.

Yes, we all agreed, that would be more than enough.

Twenty of us arrive with the Commandant in the town that evening. Huge crowds are going into the church.

'Where are you from?' the usher at the door asks the Commandant.

'We are from Poland, we are on our way home from Siberia,' she says.

The usher smiles, 'You are very welcome, please come in,' he says.

We find a space to stand in the packed church. As the Midnight Mass service on Christmas Eve in Bethlehem begins, I look round and see shining eyes and expressions of joy and serenity on the faces of those around me. The congregation is invited to join in singing 'Silent Night' in their own language. It brings back memories of long ago singing it at church with my parents. I thank God for delivering us from enslavement and for giving us this privilege that none of us ever imagined possible, of celebrating the occasion in this very special place. It was the most treasured gift amidst the mountains of grief.

Chapter 6

After our stay in Palestine, we cross the Sinai Peninsula overland in army trucks into Egypt and are stationed north of Cairo, where we set up camp in Qassassin in preparation for our transfer to Europe. Our stay in Egypt is fairly short. The allied forces are eager for the II Corps to join the fighting in Europe as are the troops themselves, who have been travelling and training for a long time. Finally, we were on our way to the frontline to fight.

We leave the great African continent, sailing out from the port of Alexandria. On the deck of the ship, my friends and I marvel at what we have seen in the Holy Land and in Egypt. My head is full of images of the land of the Pharaohs that I have only ever read about and seen sketches of. We were taken for a day to Cairo. Now I have seen for myself the wonders of the Great Pyramids of Giza and the Sphinx.

The warm sea wind blows across my face, dripping traces of salty water on my cheeks, as if to cleanse away all that I am leaving behind: the time in a nameless place, somewhere in the vastness of Siberia, where I fell in love and left a part of me, the journey across exotic lands through intriguing places: Yangi-Yul and Samarkand; mysterious countries I had never heard of: Uzbekistan, Kirghizstan and Tadzhikistan, in Asia. And the crowning jewel of Holy Mass in Bethlehem.

I don't want to forget it, not any of it, not even the terrible parts. It's all part of me now. What Father and Mother said was true.

'This will all pass. We love you. Be brave. Never give up.'

They were right. The experience of Siberia is far behind us now in time and place. I think of my parents' wedding photograph, I carry it in my heart.

'Things will get better,' they said. And now we were sailing to Europe. Every day we were getting nearer to home.

'I will be looking after you all the time,' Papa had said.

'I will find you,' Alex said.

The rocking of the ship, the touch of the soothing sun and thoughts of Bethlehem and my parents triggered memories of Christmas back home, in another time, in another world, when I was a child, in 1929.

Christmas in Poland was a magical time. The family, Mother, Father, the five of us, and Kasia and Piotr would all be sitting around the beautifully decorated

Christmas tree that Father and Adam had cut down from the farmstead and brought back to the house. We spent the whole day setting up the tree and decorating it. The fresh, pine smell oozing from the tree, permeating the entire house with the special smell of Christmas. We all joined in the decorating. Coloured baubles of red, green, silver and gold twinkled as they reflected light from the flickering, lanterns on the tree and the candles placed all along the mantelpiece and on the dining table. Strings of multicoloured glass beads, paper angels and ribbons wound garland-like around the tree, adding further layers of sparkle. The roaring fire in the hearth spitting and crackling, created a warm glow and filled the air with a scented, woody smell.

Under the tree stood the manger and all the figures of the nativity scene. Leon and I loved placing the figures in the wooden stable that Father had made. It had to be done at the right time, on the right day. Kazik passed down the ordered sequence of events to us, which he in turn had been taught by Genia and she by Adam. It would start with the empty stable, then the angel over the door and the star, then Mary and Joseph would arrive. On Christmas Eve, late at night or early on Christmas morning, the baby Jesus appeared in the manger, followed by the shepherds and their sheep. It was almost complete. Finally, on the sixth of January, the three Kings made their arrival, with their entourage and camels.

On Christmas Eve, all was set for that holy night. We prepared the special meatless, Vigil meal, 'Wigilja' consisting of 13 dishes, one representing Jesus and each of his 12 apostles. Pickled herring, *barszcz*, (beetroot soup) *uszka*, (vegetarian, pasta-filled shells), carp in aspic, salad, and everyone's favourite – *pierogi*, (dumplings) filled traditionally with mushrooms and cabbage and more with curd cheese and potato and other dishes. Then, sitting round the tree, we'd sing carols: 'Silent Night' and the 'Lullaby for Jesus'. Anna's eyes would shine, she would be beaming, while playing the enchanting harpsichord that Michal had bought for her from the church when the parish were replacing it with a new one. Adam played the guitar. Kazik, Leon and I took turns on the glockenspiel. The sound of the singing '*Lulaj że Jezuniu, lulaj że lulaj*' Rock a bye baby Jesus, rock a bye, would fill the house and drift faintly through the tightly-closed windows, so that any passer-by out in the cold, could hear the soft melodies and gentle carolling.

'Never give up…Things will get better.' I know now, you have to believe that. You have to have faith. The alternative is despair.

It takes several days to make the Mediterranean Sea crossing from Egypt to Italy. We sail close along the coast of North Africa avoiding Crete from where German bombers could strike. It is only the second time I have seen the sea. It seems much larger than the Caspian and takes much longer to cross. Once we leave the African coast and head northwards, the sea becomes rough. Huge swells and deep troughs result in many being seasick. To add to this unfamiliar experience, we are in a place where no land is visible at all. But there will be.

Chapter 7

1944

We arrive today from Alexandria in Taranto, a port in southern Italy. We travel across a countryside filled with spreading olive trees and the smell of lemons to the training camp near San Basilio, between Taranto and Bari. Serious training begins as we await orders from the allies and General Anders.

One chill morning, a couple of weeks after our arrival, we were ordered to line up outside. A group of officers was advancing towards us.

The Commanding Officer looked concerned; his gaunt features ashen. As he walked past me, I noticed his eyes glistening. He looked around at the rows of soldiers in front of him as if gauging his audience. After a moment, he began to speak. He talked of the atrocities of war. He confirmed the rumours we had heard about the horrors of mass killings in German concentration camps. He spoke about 'Man's inhumanity to man.' It seemed like something more was yet to come, as if he was preparing us.

He began to tell us what happened to thousands of Polish soldiers, officers and members of the intelligentsia who had been slaughtered. He had no names of the victims. No one had, as no such list existed, he said. I felt a thud in the pit of my stomach at the mention of 'Polish officers.' Adam, my beloved brother Adam. What had happened to him? I had not seen or heard from him since the first day of the deportation. Had he been taken away because he was an officer in the Polish army? And what had happened to Leon and Kazik?

The Commanding Officer continued. He said that some of us may remember or may have heard how all communication from Polish officers and members of the intelligentsia to their families had suddenly ceased. For three years, approximately from April 1940 to 1943, families had no contact with their loved ones, and they had no idea what had happened to them.

He told us that on the 12th April 1943, the Germans announced in the media that they had made a gruesome discovery in Russia. In the depths of a forest, near Smolensk, at a place called Katyń, the Germans had found mass graves of what turned out to be Polish officers and military personnel. The mass graves included civilians, some of whom had been identified from identity papers left on them.[1] Among them were doctors, political activists, writers, teachers, professors and other members of the intellectual elite.

The Commanding Officer paused. There was a stunned silence. I thought of Adam. Had he been killed there? I tried to stifle my wail. Numerous others in the ranks looked distressed. Emotion was only just contained behind the swelling dam.

After a few more moments, the Commanding Officer said that he was going to describe how they died. Anyone who wished to leave at that point could do so. Not one person left. He told us that the victims were forced to kneel at the edge of a pit with their hands tied behind their back. They were then shot in the back of the head. Those who resisted were gagged and had their greatcoats pulled over their heads and tied with a rope around their necks, which was connected to their hands behind their back in a choke knot. The result of this was that any struggle at all meant the rope round their neck would tighten and so with each movement, they would come closer to self-strangulation.[2] The alternative course of action of keeping still and not trying to escape avoided strangulation but resulted in an interminably slow death amidst a heap of dying bodies and corpses.

The dam burst and flooded the field. Some of the soldiers listening to this abhorrent account, fell to the ground, calling out names of loved ones who had disappeared. Others fainted from shock. I could only think that Adam was among the slaughtered helpless, and worse still, that Kazik and Leon had also suffered the same despicable fate. All three brothers could have died there.

The Commanding Officer opened a document wallet that he had been holding, and revealed more details of one of the burial pits and the numbers of Polish officers in one mass grave. He read out that the pit was, '28 metres long and 16 metres wide, filled with 12 layers of bodies of Polish officers, numbering about 3,000. All of them had wounds in the back of their necks caused by pistol shots.'[2]

The CO told us that the mass graves were discovered on 12th April 1943 by the Germans, who reported what they found to the German press. Their findings were transmitted to the international press. An outcry had erupted calling for those responsible to be brought to justice. But just as the Germans blamed the Russians for the atrocity, the Russians denied culpability and blamed the Germans for perpetrating the barbaric crime.

There was more that he wanted us to know about what had happened to the deportees and POWs who were still detained in Russia. Two things had changed the course of events. The first was that in January 1943, the Polish Government refused to accept the Curzon Line as the Polish-Russian border. Secondly, the Polish Government's reaction to the Katyń crime, believing the Russians were to blame, angered Stalin. The two events had resulted in Stalin revoking the

1941 Amnesty on 25 April 1943. This was disastrous for those left behind, a number far greater than those who had already been evacuated. Over 25,000 who had received amnesty documents in the last months of 1941 and Polish passports were forced to return both to the Russian authorities. Others who refused to sign documents agreeing to Russian citizenship, were imprisoned or tried and sent to the Gulags for two to five years. From that time, no one had been allowed to leave the Soviet Union.[3]

How could we know any more about our relatives? There was no list of the victims. All we could do was pray for our loved ones and for all the victims. I refuse to accept that I might never see Adam, Kazik and Leon again.

Chapter 8

After the deaths of Mother and Father, Adam became very important to me. He took the place of both my parents. He was a kind and loving guardian and a father figure to all of us left behind. He told me much later that he was concerned about me as I was so young when we experienced the trauma of our parents' deaths. A special bond developed between us.

I remember one day when I was about eight years old, Adam and I went to the forest, as we often did, to pick blueberries to make preserves and to use for cooking.

'You are the chief berry-picker,' Adam said, 'I'm just assisting.' He would always accompany me to protect me from the wild boars that roamed the forests or any other dangers. He carried a rifle and we rode there together on horseback.

When we got there that day, we tied the horse to a tree and started walking into the woods. I was carrying two baskets for the berries. We had done this many times before. We were walking and chatting but that time, Adam was unusually quiet. I didn't know why then, but now I think he might have been thinking about Katarina, they were seeing each other a lot then. As we went further into the woods, we heard a strange sound. It was a rustling noise followed by a soft flapping. We edged towards where the sound was coming from. A few steps later we saw it was a tiny bird, caught in an animal trap, its foot clamped by the metal bar. There it was, struggling for freedom, its fearful eyes pleading for help. Adam crouched down and gently put his hand on the poor bird. He held it in the palm of his hand, carefully and securely. With his other hand, he was holding the metal trap. He told me to press a lever which opened the trap to release the innocent victim. I did, but the bird hardly moved. Adam clasped it in both hands and I stroked its head gently. Blood was dripping from the injured limb. I wiped it with the corner of my apron. Setting the bird down on the forest floor, we watched it as it wobbled a little, tripped over a protruding tree root and finally managed to stand upright. Hopping precariously amongst the leaves, it eventually managed to move fast enough to flap its wings and fly.

I was so relieved that it was able to fly. I can still remember what Adam said when he looked at me and smiled.

'Yes, with just a little love and care, we can all survive even the most life-threatening circumstances, even when we think we're going to die and there seems to be no hope.' His words mean so much more to me now than they did then.

Everything was calm again in the forest. We spent all morning picking the abundant crop of blueberries. We filled the two baskets and used my apron and headscarf to collect the glut of berries. Our hands and mouths were stained dark purple from the irresistible crop.

'Look at your face,' said Adam laughing.

'And yours.'

Exhausted, we sat down on the forest floor in the tiny clearing to have our lunch. I looked up at the canopy of trees. Out of the corner of my eye, I caught a slight movement and sensed a presence watching us. I turned and signalled to Adam. He stopped moving, and in the silent stillness of the forest, I could make out the faint sound of gentle, rhythmic breathing. I turned around. There face to face with us stood the most enormous, majestic stag. It was very near, no more than ten metres from us. It was perfectly still, like a statue. We had not heard anything to signal its approach. I remember thinking, how strange that was, as it was such a huge creature. The only movement was its nostrils dilating as its breathing appeared to quicken. Its large eyes, looked the colour of a menacingly dangerous lake as they reflected the forest colours. The creature stared directly at us, motionless. I was a captive, transfixed by its regal presence. I gazed at its magnificent face and sculpted antlers. It was both beautiful and terrifying; vulnerable and threatening. In a flash, it could have trampled over us in a panic to escape back into the depths of the forest. Adam could have shot it straight away to defend us but he would not have wanted to harm it. There it stood staring at us with an air of aloofness.

'What right do you have to be here on my territory?' it seemed to be saying.

Then just as suddenly as it had appeared, its ears pricked up, it quivered. Perhaps it had heard a branch snap under the foot of some distant forest animal. It darted effortlessly, with all the energy and elegance of a ballet dancer, back from wherever it had come.

I couldn't believe what we had just seen, so close to us. I was going to treasure the memories of the bird and the stag and I couldn't wait to tell my friends, Mila and Julcia, all about it.

Chapter 9

1944-1945

The words of an Officer spoken on the day we move towards Monte Cassino.

'On a hilltop, approximately eighty-eight miles south east of the eternal city of Rome, stands the hilltop monastery of Monte Cassino, the German stronghold, where we are heading today to join the allies at the front to defeat the enemy. The front – the Gustav line – runs south of Monte Cassino, across the Italian peninsula from west to east.'

Thoughts of Katyń still fresh in our minds, we enter a land enclosed by mountains, ridges, steep-sided walls of rock; claustrophobic in their effect. Hard and permanent, so different to the soft, changing desert sands. At base level, tortuous river valleys encircle each hill with its own moat-like defence. A few precarious roads and tracks snake their way through the terrain. We drive as far as it is possible to get the trucks along.

I take turns with Tomas to drive the truck we are assigned to.

I learned to drive when we were stationed in Iraq. I had asked Commandant Bronisława if I could practice on the army trucks there. She was a little hesitant at first but I think I surprised her by how keen I was. When I said that if I learned to drive, I'd be able to transport the injured to hospital and get supplies for the camp, she must have seen some sense in my reasoning and ordered an experienced driver, Tomas, to oversee my training. After several hair-raising attempts, I was in control of the vehicle. I was thrilled to pass the military driving test first time and have been driving unaccompanied whenever needed ever since.

Our cargo in Italy is troops and ammunition. The terrain is rough and unpredictable. The untarmacked roads are narrow and, in places, non-existent or strewn with boulders. We reach a bend that almost doubles back on itself, proving difficult to manoeuvre the truck round it.

'Sharp turn Zosia, full lock on,' says Tomas.

'Yes, done sir.'

'Back the 'beast' up and try again.'

'Yes, sir.' It takes a number of tries. The 'beast' is large and bulky and the turn very tight. Something about 'getting a camel through the eye of a needle,'[1] springs to mind. The only godsend is that there are no precipitous drops on either side, as we are in the valley. After reversing four or five times, I manage to get the truck round the bend. There are several more of these tight bends.

After the last one, as if by way of reward, the most unexpected sight appears. We stare at the spectacular beauty which rears up in front of us. On top of the highest mountain that we have seen so far, is the monumental, Benedictine monastery of Monte Cassino. The sight of immense walls, luminescent in the glaring sun, together with endless lines of windows, dazzling as we get nearer, is overwhelming. A testament to faith in the most impenetrable of places. Built on top of a vast crag, on all sides, surrounded by steep slopes, enclosed by rivers, separating this bastion from the next ridge of mountains, which follows the same impenetrable pattern.

'It was founded in AD 529,' says Tomas, reading from a booklet about Italy.

'How on earth did they manage to build anything in such an inaccessible place?'

'I have no idea, Zosia. I can't begin to fathom it. According to this, the present monastery was built much later in the eleventh century.'

'That is still unbelievable.'

We set up camp in distant view of the monastery, and through the night we hear the sound of continuous shelling and artillery fire.

At our briefing, we learn that the monastery was occupied by the Germans in the latter part of 1943. It has an important strategic position: on the Gustav

Line and south east of the Italian capital. Occupation of the citadel prevents the Allies from reaching and defending Rome.

The Battle of Monte Cassino, or the Battle for Rome, started in December 1943 with minor assaults on the monastery. From the 17th January 1944, the Allies made further attempts to capture the citadel, but without success, due not only to the impenetrability of the geographical terrain but to the defence strategy of the Germans. Three major battles took place from January 1944, involving a wide range of allied troops: Moroccans, Indians and New Zealanders and other Commonwealth forces.

Then the unthinkable happened. Despite strong opposition between the Allies, the controversial order to destroy the citadel is agreed. Having failed to capture the stronghold by land, an air attack is instigated. 1,400 tons of explosives are deployed on the monastery by bombers. It is completely destroyed. However, the enemy does not surrender. Instead, they maintain their position more strongly amidst the rubble of the decimated citadel. Mist and smoke blur the ruined outline of what remains after the devastation of the air assault. We wait eagerly for orders to join the Allies in the fight.

Rumours about Poland are spreading through the ranks. We hear German radio broadcasting information on a station called, 'Wanda' in Polish about plans for post-war Poland. The programme says that agreement was reached about Poland's future at a Conference in Tehran in November 1943 between Britain, America and Russia. It will come under Soviet control at the end of the war. As well as this, the Curzon Line will form the eastern frontier with Russia. The Germans know that this would be devastating for those in the II Corps, as most of us, are from eastern Poland. It means our homes would no longer be part of Poland. They would become part of Russia, and the rest of Poland would be under Russian control.

When we learned about what had happened in Katyń, our feelings sank deep into despair. We did not imagine it could get any worse. In an effort to lower morale further, the Germans are dropping leaflets from aircraft, about the Katyń genocide, written in Polish, so that as we prepare for battle, we can be reminded of what our Russian allies have done. They know that many of us have relatives who could be among the Katyń victims. This, and the broadcasts are the Germans' way of wearing down their enemy, and to some extent both succeed.

Here we are in the hinterland of the insurmountable Monte Cassino. Spirits are indescribably low. Do we care what happens here now?

General Anders releases his orders.

'If we do capture Monte Cassino, and capture it we must, then we will bring Poland's cause – currently so hard-pressed – to the fore of world opinion.'[2]

Had it not been for his words and everyone's strong sense of duty and honour, some of us may have given up.

We enter into battle, all the more determined to overcome the hitherto invincible enemy. We need to prove ourselves. We have not yet been involved in any fighting since our release. The British wanted us moved from Iraq to be actively deployed in Europe. We are determined to demonstrate our worth, despite the odds and despite the rumours of collaboration between the Western Allies and the Soviet Union.

In Monte Cassino, every artillery and infantry soldier is to be mobilised to the front line if we are to stand any chance of succeeding in overthrowing the enemy. I find myself driving ammunition trucks to the front line, along with some of the other women drivers recently trained. We seem to be a novelty; they call us the *'driverki', (female drivers)*. We are honoured to play our part. I drive from the temporary munition stores to the front, on my own in the truck, driving back and forth for days across the obstructive terrain through a barrage of gunfire. Compared to the men ascending the mount, my task is easy. Capturing the stronghold is far from straightforward as the earlier failed attempts demonstrate. It is becoming even more the case due to the number of injured troops. Casualties who make it back to the base are loaded onto the trucks and we drive them to hospital tents on the way back to the munition stations. The way is strewn with the remnants of vehicles destroyed by mines. That was the first couple of days.

There are reports that General Anders is devastated by the numbers of casualties and losses. The remaining troops are to rest for five days to regain their strength. In that time, he flies over the fortress and we are informed of the German strategy which he discovers. They are employing a figure of eight line of defence, which gives them a 360-degree view of any attempted assaults on the mount.

There is to be a renewed attack. The aim is to break up the uninterrupted view the enemy has. This time there would be a two-pronged attack from different sides of the mountain, forcing the Germans to defend two areas simultaneously, thus halving their defence in any one place at any given time.

The Polish soldiers crawl up the hillside on their bellies, carrying grenades and ammunition. Saddled with the maximum possible, around thirty grenades each, they are heavily weighed down. We deliver large amounts of ammunition as quickly as possible from early morning till night. To make it worse, the steep terrain they are climbing up, offers very little cover, no trees or bushes, just bare rocks. Many of these have been shattered by enemy artillery shells from earlier attempts to defend the fortress. The smoke-filled air and the smell of putrefied decay chokes the soldiers as they make their brave ascent. On the ground underfoot, in any slight dip in the slope, lie heaps of corpses of the previous assailants.

The troops attack together with the British and other allies and break part of one of the defence rings on the northern side. Finally, that night, the Germans admit defeat and withdraw from the obliterated monastery on 17th May 1944.

The following morning, a small group of allied soldiers enter the monastery. Finding it abandoned, they raise a Polish flag over the hollow ruins and a lancer plays the Kraków 'Hejnał.'[3]

The allies are triumphant at last. Following the jubilation, we transfer to different parts of Italy, fighting with the allies in Ancona to defeat the Germans. Then on to northern Italy where the enemy has occupied the town of Bologna. We fight again and succeed in defeating the enemy on the 21st of April, 1945. The repeated German surrenders in Italy signal the end of the war is in sight. We are inching closer and closer to peace and to returning home.

But, against this backdrop, we learn from one of the Commanding Officers about the Yalta agreement in February 1945. This time it is not a rumour. This time it confirms what we feared and what the alleged, Tehran discussions had in fact been about. At Yalta, the three political leaders of the US, Britain and the Soviet Union, Roosevelt, Churchill and Stalin, have agreed that the borders of post-war Poland are to be realigned. The area of Poland east of the Curzon Line is to become part of Russia. It will no longer belong to Poland. This is all of eastern Poland, where the majority of the Polish II Corps originate from. The Commanding Officer informs us that:

'After all the suffering and death, that somewhere in the region of one to two million innocent people[4] have undergone over the last five years and eight months, our homes are no longer part of the free Poland we have all dreamed of returning to one day; it will belong to the Soviet Union. And that is not all,' he says.

'The Government of Poland is to come under the control of the Soviet Union who will oversee not only our elections but also the selection of candidates.'

Gasps are followed by silence. Any euphoria we should be feeling about defeating the enemy and the prospect of the end of the war, are wiped out by the news.

A message from General Anders is read out:

'We will continue to liberate towns and villages, to carry out bloody battles, because all roads lead to Poland. And this Poland is closer and closer but so desperately distant.'[5]

Following these revelations, General Anders flies to Britain for discussions with the British Government. We learn that the decisions about post-war Poland were made without including any representatives from Poland or considering the views of its citizens. Later we are told the outcome of his talks by the CO.

'At the moment, there are no changes to the Yalta agreement. It stands. It seems that keeping favour with the new Russian ally is the priority.'

Morale reaches a critically low point. There is a strong feeling, among the troops, that we have been betrayed by our allies. Polish armed forces have fought with the allies, and now those same allies have agreed to the annexation of eastern Poland and to post-war Soviet control of the country.

This is not the outcome we ever imagined for the future of our beloved '*ojczyzna*', (fatherland). Our country's government will be under Soviet control and our homes are no longer in Poland. Both are in the hands of those who invaded our country and deported us. Those who said that they had come to save us, but instead enslaved us. Those who said they were our friends but turned out to be our enemy, then became our ally and now? Who and what should we trust? What now for our country and our homes? And what hope for a free Poland?

Part 5

The Ending

Chapter 1

My Journal, 1991

When the war ended, I was in Italy, near Bologna. It was the 8th May 1945. They called it 'Victory in Europe Day' or 'VE Day.' In the morning the news broke. It was hard to take in that the war was finally over, after almost six long years.

We were outside, lined up as usual for the morning briefing. I remember when the announcement was made, the troops exploded into a riot of cheering. They were jumping up and down, shouting out with excitement. Everyone joined in. We were hugging and kissing whoever we were next to. For the first time since the deportation, we couldn't stop grinning and laughing with joy. Only later did I realise how naïve we were.

No duties that day. We were free to do whatever we wanted.

My friends and most of the II Corps decided to walk into the centre of Bologna. The first sound of celebrations reached us as we came over the brow of the hill. We could hear music and cheering. Entering the town, we were met by the Italians and allied troops who were already celebrating in the streets. There was singing and dancing. Everyone had a smile on their face and the sound of laughter could be heard in the streets. Women and children were running up to us and thrusting flowers into our hands. The locals were hugging and kissing anyone in army uniform, thanking them for helping to liberate their country. There were tables outside with whatever food and drink they had for everyone. We joined in the dancing and tried to sing the Italian songs. Peace in Europe had been restored at long last.

Later that same day, Eva, Sabina, Hanka and I walked through the town centre. We reached a shady square that provided some respite from the midday heat and crowds. I remember the strong, vanilla-like scent that hung in the air, from the pink and white flowering shrubs cascading from the pergolas. Beneath them, there were benches for any passers-by. We saw groups of allied soldiers sitting there. Among them Stan, Paweł and Janusz chatting together. We joined them on the benches.

We were so excited. It was wonderful to see all the happy faces and people laughing and dancing. We hadn't seen anything like that for a very long time, not since before the invasions of 1939. Of course, in everyone's mind was the thought that it would not be long before we would be going home.

But some were sceptical about the prospect. Paweł said that it was not going to be straightforward. We would have to wait and see what the politicians decided. It would depend partly on whether or not they changed their minds about the Yalta decisions. None of us knew the answers.

We were hopeful, especially in view of the part that our armies had played throughout Europe to help defeat the enemy. Like any country, Poland had a right to its independence and to its rightful borders being restored.

Paweł had said that our role at Monte Cassino had been critical to the outcome. Without Anders's strategy, the allies would still be crawling up that 'monster of a mountain and be getting slaughtered like helpless lambs.' After all the time of unjustified exile and wanderings across the globe, it was time for us to go back to the homeland that we all yearned for so much.

At that moment, in my mind's eye, I could see it: the farmstead and the golden fields. I saw Father, Mother and Adam around the hearth. The wedding photo we had left behind, was still propped up against the clock. I longed to hold it. I longed to be there with them, to touch them, to hug and kiss them.

In slow motion and silently, I pictured Papa and me riding on his horse together, bathed in sunlight, the red ribbon on my hat floating in the air behind me, moments before it was snatched away.

Then, it was almost as if Paweł could see my thoughts, he was talking about walking over the Austrian Alps, through Hungary and Czechoslovakia to Poland. He said we could reach it on foot in several months. It wasn't far, around nine hundred to a thousand miles to Lwów. It wasn't any different to some of the distances we had covered on foot in the Soviet Union.

It was such a tempting idea. How near we were. It was perfectly possible. It would be much warmer and more hospitable than what we had experienced in the USSR. And with such a goal in sight, it would seem even nearer.

But Stan and others said that it was not safe to go then. He said that they would have to wait for the politicians to decide the future of Poland. If they didn't change their minds about the Yalta Agreement, it would be disastrous. Anyone who left then, would be in Poland, but it wouldn't be the country they knew and loved. It would be under Soviet control. For most of us, who came from east of the Curzon Line, our homes wouldn't even be in Poland anymore. He said that they would probably shoot us or, our worst nightmare, send us back to Siberia. They didn't want us there. That's why they had deported us in the first place. There was no choice but to wait. We couldn't risk being 'sent back to the Polar Bears,' as Janusz used to say. None of us wanted that. We had to wait for answers which would decide our future. We had no idea how long it would take for the politicians to resolve the situation. It seemed so near and yet it was beyond our reach.

I remember seeing pictures of celebrations across Europe in the newspapers. There was one of the King of England, George VI, the Queen Consort, Elizabeth, the Princesses Elizabeth and Margaret on the balcony of a beautiful building, called Buckingham Palace waving to ecstatic crowds crammed into the avenues in front of it. There were more pictures of victory celebrations and jubilant people in Paris, Lisbon and New York.

* * *

This story I have to include in my journal because it is about a very special person who would change the next part of my life forever. It happened in Northern Europe in 1945. Its effects turned out to be very significant not only to the war but also to many people, and to me personally.

It was during one of the most important battles, which took place in Germany, just before the end of the war. It happened along the northern shores of Europe, near a place called Wilhelmshaven.

At the same time as the defeat of the enemy in the Italian city of Bologna, in April 1945, another distinct part of the Polish Army, the First Polish Armoured Regiment, was stationed in Northern Europe. The

Armoured Regiment were engaged in France and Germany, having previously spent time in Scotland training and defending potential entry points to the UK from invasion. The Division consisted of 13,000 men, including officers, 381 tanks, 473 artillery pieces and 3050 vehicles on 1st August 1943. [1]

They set sail from Southampton to France. Their aim was to prevent the advancement of the German forces. The Division was stationed in Normandy and moved along parts of the coast from Caen through Belgium, to Breda in the Netherlands and as far as the strategic German naval port of Wilhelmshaven; a total distance of some 1,125 miles.

Back in late October, 1944, they were engaged in battle and lost a number of their men, including a young cadet, called Michułka. While on lookout, he put his head out of the tank to get a better view and was killed by enemy fire. The following morning, on the 29th October, the soldiers were cleaning their equipment and the inside of the tank following the death of their compatriot. They were in shock from the death of their friend who died in their midst in their tank.

While they were trying to come to terms with the senseless death of Michułka and others, supplies were being delivered: petrol, ammunition and provisions. The 'yard' was very busy with trucks delivering and unloading. The officer in charge, Major Bartosiński inspected the ranks as usual as he did every morning and uttered words of kindness to the soldiers who had lost men from their corps.

Kazimierz Nowak was one of the drivers of the tank in which Michułka was killed. Kazimierz and his friends in the Regiment[2] were deeply affected by Michułka's death and walked around in dazed disbelief carrying out their orders. Kazimierz was checking and collecting the petrol delivery. Provisions were arriving and were being collected by the Regiment's cooks. Everyone was helping to make sure the delivery was as smooth and efficient as possible amidst the threat of surprise shelling from the enemy.

Kazimierz picked up four empty petrol cannisters, two in each hand, to take back to the petrol tanker. As he was carrying them, Major Bartosiński told Kazimierz to give the cannisters to him. He would take them back. He ordered Kazimierz to instruct the others to get the tanks ready for action, urgently.

The Major took the petrol cannisters back to the tanker. At precisely the moment that they took their first steps in opposite directions to each other, there was a barrage of heavy firing from enemy lines. Kazimierz dropped to the ground immediately. He could hear the bullets whistling over his head. This was followed by an explosion and the thud of someone falling. Someone had taken a hit. He looked up, to where the last noise had come from and could not believe his eyes. The Major had been hit. Major Bartosiński had taken a direct artillery hit to his left side, in all probability straight to the heart. He was killed instantly.

That was the last enemy fire at the camp that morning. They were all devastated that the Major had been killed and that it had happened so quickly. Kazimierz could not take in what had just happened. He couldn't help wondering if he had taken the cannisters himself, would he have been hit, would he have been the one lying dead on the ground now instead of the Major. But he thought he would probably have moved faster with the cannisters than the Major and that the same bullet would not have reached him. Also, he would not have been in that exact place, as by his estimation, he would have passed that point sooner had the Major not stopped him for those few split seconds to give him his orders. But the enemy must have been aiming. In all probability, they had targeted the Major. But he would never know for sure. Whatever thoughts streamed through his head, he knew for certain, that by some amazing stroke of fate, he had had a very lucky escape indeed.[3]

In April 1945, the First Armoured Division, nicknamed 'The Black Devils', were under orders to fulfil the objective of capturing the important German Naval Base of Wilhelmshaven. The battle lasted from 19th to 29th April 1945 and along with the allied forces they succeeded in overwhelming and defeating the Naval Base. The enemy agreed to the only option on offer:

unconditional surrender. The First Armoured Division was charged with overseeing the submission of a German General, an Admiral and nineteen thousand German officers. In addition, the Division was put in control of the huge number of ships, submarines, other vessels, artillery and weaponry in the Base.[1] The Battle at Wilhelmshaven was one of the last battles of the war.

The day after it ended, on the 30th April, Hitler committed suicide in his Berlin bunker. Germany surrendered unconditionally to the Allies on 2nd May 1945.

In June 1946, more than a year after the VE Day celebrations, we were still in Italy waiting for the outcome of discussions which would decide our future. Could we go back to Poland or would we have to wait? And if we couldn't go back, what were we going to do?

Commandant Bronisława addressed us about the predicament we were all in. She said that the safest option was to stay with the army and wait for news. None of us had any money for food or transport anywhere. But the army would take care of us, feed us, house us and get us to the right place, a safe place.

It had become clear that the decisions made in Tehran and reconfirmed at Yalta in 1945 between the big three, Roosevelt, Churchill and Stalin were not going to change. There was little or no choice over what to do. There were two questions, she said that we needed to ask ourselves:

Firstly, did we want to go back to a Poland under the imposed communist regime, to the possible consequences of life under Soviet control? We had to realise that it was far from safe and that there could be further deportations.

And secondly, for those of us whose homes were east of the Curzon Line, did we want to return to what was now officially part of the Soviet Union? We would almost certainly have to accept Soviet citizenship.

There was one other option. There had been discussion about compensation for the lands lost in eastern Poland, in the form of lands in the west, formerly German territory, being given to Poland. Resettlement would be possible there. The Commandant knew that this could not possibly compensate for the loss of our homes, and it would, of course, be under Soviet control.

The strong advice was to remain with the army for as long as necessary, until safe haven could be obtained. Returning to Poland at the current time was dangerous, anyone who did so, would be taking a great risk.

Numbers in the army increased as Polish men from western Poland, who had been forcibly conscripted to the German army at the beginning of the war, were leaving and joining the II Corps in Italy. At that time, there were over 100,000 troops.

Finally, agreement was reached between Commander Anders and the British Government to move Polish exiles to Britain. From the 85,000 troops who came out of the Soviet Union with Anders, around 300 individuals chose to return to Poland. From June to October 1946, the rest of us set out on the journey to Britain.

England, 1946-7

We were housed in the new Resettlement Camps which opened in 1947. We believed that this was a temporary arrangement until it was safe for us to return to Poland.

The Resettlement Camps were old army camps, used during the war by American and Canadian troops. But they were nothing like the barracks in Siberia. These had electricity, heating and lighting. There were bathrooms with hot and cold running water. We found ourselves somewhere in the middle of England, in unpronounceable parts of the country called, 'Gloucestershire' and 'Warwickshire.'

It wasn't long before we began training in a range of skills to equip us for civilian life and employment. I learned to use a sewing machine and trained as a seamstress. We had English Language lessons, as very few of us knew any English at all.

I was with Eva, Sabina and Hanka, and our group of friends grew. It included Stan, Paweł, Janusz and others from the labour camp and those met on the journey out of the Siberian camps. We spent nearly two years in the Resettlement Camps, waiting and hoping for an opportunity to return home, while we were being prepared for an independent, civilian existence.

News about what had happened to some of the soldiers and exiles returning to Poland reached us. There were executions. Some of those returning from the II Corps were deported once more to Siberia. Returning Russian soldiers were also being executed in the Soviet Union. As for General Anders, he had been denied Polish citizenship and was stripped of his military rank by the communist controlled government in Poland.

Shortly before we left the Resettlement Camps, we were instructed not to speak about our experience in Siberia and not to talk about anything related to the Soviet Union with British people.

We thought it strange. We didn't know why they had told us not to speak about Siberia. We could not see how we could not talk about what we had been through, or understand how they could expect us to keep it secret. It was impossible. We couldn't just wipe it from our minds, even though, in some ways, we would have liked to. We took comfort in the fact that at least, we could talk about it between ourselves. Perhaps we should try to forget what happened. But I don't think we can ever forget it. I don't think we should.

London, 1948

We were pleased to leave the Resettlement Camps and eager to start living our own independent lives at long last. The army wages we were being paid, meant that we had a little money to survive on until we could find work. As soon as possible, we moved to London. The three girls and I rented a cheap flat together and started looking for work.

On Sunday, we went to a Polish mass in a church in central London. I still remember the Polish priest's sermon which started with the words, '*Forgive us our trespasses, as we forgive those who trespass against us.*' [4]

He told us we had to forgive and strive to create a new life for ourselves. We were lucky to have survived. We should remember and pray for the millions from every nation who had perished in the war. To forgive was to let go and set ourselves free.

At communion, I saw two young girls with flaxen hair walking down the aisle. My heart stopped. They looked like Juzia and Lucia. I looked round for Genia and Wojtek. The girls seemed to be on their own. They turned round to walk back from communion and my heart sank when I saw that they were not my nieces.

There were organisations putting people in touch with separated family members. Lists of names were posted outside the church. We searched for our missing families but without luck. More lists went up daily, and we continued to search through them.

Then one day, I spotted the name 'Leon Błaszczyk' and an address. My brother. He was alive and in London. Eva and I went to the address straight away. No one was in, so we waited for Leon to arrive. We thought that he must be at work. Sure enough, not long after six o'clock, he came striding down the road. I recognised his unmistakable gait. I ran towards him.

'Zosia, is that you?' he shouted as he was running towards me. He lifted me off the ground and spun me round. I was so happy to see him. Still the same Leon, though a little older and more worn.

We spent the whole evening talking. He told me that he and Kazik had been together during the war and that Kazik was living in a house in north London. Genia, Wojtek and the children were staying with him. We decided to go the next day to see them. I could barely sleep that night with excitement. There was no phone in their house to let them know we were coming. We were just going to turn up.

When we got there, we could see the girls sitting on the wall outside the house reading and chatting. They shrieked with delight when they saw me and Leon approaching and ran towards us.

'Aunty Zosia! Aunty Zosia!' they were shouting.

Juzia, Lucia, my darling nieces. They had no idea how happy I was to see them. We were hugging and kissing. What young ladies they had become. Lucia was thirteen, and Juzia was fifteen. I remember thinking that, Juzia was the same age as I was when we left Poland. It was a long time since I had last seen them. It must have been six or seven years ago when they were leaving the camp on the sledge.

Then the girls pointed at a boy walking down the road towards us. It was Antoni, they told me. I would never have recognised him. The last time I had seen him, he was a toddler. He gave me a hug and a kiss and told me he was ten. Hearing the excitement, Genia and Wojtek came out of the house.

'Zosia! Thank God, you're safe,' said Genia. More hugs and kisses from them. We went inside the house. Kazik was not back from work yet. Genia asked how we had found them. I told her how we had seen Leon's name on the lists outside the church but had not seen their names. Genia explained that they had only just arrived in London a few days ago. But no one had any news of Adam.

Lucia told me that they had been taken to India. They stayed in a large house and there was a school. It belonged to an Indian Maharaja who had given it for Polish orphans, mothers and children released from the Soviet Union to use. It was beautiful, like a palace. He was a very kind man, she said. Genia said that they had been very lucky to have gone there and would always be grateful for the generosity of the Maharaja whose name was Jam Saheb Digvijay of Sinhji. But Wojtek had not been with them. He was conscripted soon after they left the camp and they hadn't seen him for the past five years, until a few days ago.

I told them about some of what happened to me and they listened with interest. Then Genia told me that they were thinking of moving to America or Canada as there seemed to be more opportunities there. She asked me to go with them. Leon was keen to go. She wasn't sure about what Kazik wanted to do as he had met an English girl. When she asked me, I did not know what I was going to do.

Not long after however, my mind was made up. There was one very special person in London that made my choice clear. In the end, I decided to stay in England. I love my family very much, and for them, it was a good idea to go to North America. But for me, the special person and all my friends were in London. Friends, who had been with me in Siberia or on the long journey back to Europe. I didn't want to leave them. We had become close through our shared experience. I was tired of travelling, and America and Canada were so much further from our homeland.

In the end, Genia and Wojtek did decide to emigrate to Canada and settled in Toronto. Leon left for America and settled in Boston. Kazik stayed in London and married Elizabeth, his English girlfriend. Both brothers had their own families. I stayed in London with my friends. There was still no news of Adam.

A few months after the family was reunited in London, in a small hall in Victoria, a Polish celebration was taking place. There was music and dance. I went with my friends, we were the new émigrés, made up of those who experienced Russian and German occupation and deportation. We were enjoying our free time, singing and dancing. The music reminded me of home and one piece, in particular, reminded me of Kasia and Piotr's wedding celebrations back in Bortków, many years ago, a long time before all the horrors of the war. Tears began to roll down my face as I remembered that lost time, that stolen life; gone forever in the shattered kaleidoscope of my past. The more I thought about it, the more the tears streamed down my face.

Then I heard a deep, tender voice say:

'Why are you crying? We've won! The war is over. Be happy to be alive. You have survived.'

I looked up. Through my tears I saw who the voice belonged to, an ex-serviceman in uniform, with the kindest face and the bluest eyes I had ever seen.

'Let me introduce myself. My name is Kazimierz Nowak, I'm delighted to meet you.'

'I'm Zofia.' He took my hand and kissed it in the traditional, gentlemanly fashion.

'Shall we dance Zofia?' And, we did, for the rest of the evening.

A long time later, he told me about his war experiences and how he was thankful to be alive, having escaped being shot by German soldiers due to an incredible stroke of luck.

Much later, I told him my story.

On St. George's Day, the 23rd April,1949, we were married in the Roman Catholic Church of Saint Peter and Saint Edward, Westminster and in the registry of Caxton Hall in London. The reception was at '*Ognisko*' the Polish 'Hearth' Club in Kensington. The guests included many of our friends who had lived through similar ordeals and hardship from 1939 until the end of the war. Our experience bonded us together. We were part of a new family, building a new life in the UK.

We received military crosses for the part we played in the war and in the fight for Monte Cassino. I was so proud of everyone who had been involved in the Battle for Rome.

General Anders was awarded the Order of the Bath by King George V1 for his significant role in the victory at Monte Cassino and in the war against Germany.

We were happy. But not about what was happening in Poland. Polish media in the UK confirmed the terrible stories about the fate of the exiles who returned to Poland. Poland was behind the Iron Curtain, under Communist control. There were no free elections and the eastern side of the country had been annexed by the Soviet Union. Those remaining there were forced to take Russian citizenship and denounce Polish nationality on pain of death.

London, 1989

For over forty years, from 1947 to 1989, we lived in exile in England. In the early years, we lived in continued hope that one day things would change and we would return home permanently. But Poland was still under Soviet control and eastern Poland as we knew it, no longer existed. It was part of Ukraine, also under Soviet control. Lwów had become Lviv. We travelled to Poland to visit Kazimierz's family in Warsaw and in the countryside outside Warsaw, as well as in the north west of Poland. He showed me the place in Warsaw where a bomb had fallen at the beginning of the war and killed his mother. We visited her grave in the vast Warsaw cemetery. But I never went back to Bortków because it was in the USSR.

We had made a new life with our friends. Our new, extended family doubled in size as we all married. Some of my friends also married soldiers from The First Armoured Regiment.[5] We all had children and by 1989, some had grandchildren, but we never forgot our homeland. We created our own Poland in England, one in which we could talk freely about our wartime experiences and our journey of over nine thousand miles from our fatherland to Siberia, through Asia and back to Europe.

Then in 1989, something happened which changed everything. The Fall of Communism took place following the dismantling of the Berlin Wall. The overthrow of Communist rule throughout Eastern Europe was complete.

It was only at that point, in 1989 that the content of the secret agreement of the partition of Poland, made in the Non-Aggression Pact and signed by Ribbentrop and Molotov, became public, fifty years after it was signed. The original cartoon of Hitler and Stalin from 1939, that I had seen in Siberia, appeared in a newspaper. There was a new one placed alongside it for the 1989 revelation. It showed the Yalta agreement. There were scrolls representing the various meetings and negotiations, with Quebec, August 1943, Tehran, November 1943 and finally Yalta, February 1945 on the table in front of Stalin. The article confirmed that the agreement had been reached much earlier than 1945. This time, a weary-looking Roosevelt, was depicted as the wolf, holding the American and United Nations flags. Churchill was sitting on the floor in front of him, depicted as a cowering bulldog with the Union Jack wound around his neck. They were shown giving Eastern Poland to a large, smiling bear wearing a cap with the name Stalin on it. There was a Russian flag on the map over Warsaw. The caption read, 'The bear got what he wanted and much more.'

1991

At the same time as the Fall of Communism, the rise of a new movement in Poland, called 'Solidarity' was taking place. Its recognition as a political party became critical. For the first time since WWII, Eastern European countries had free democratic elections. In Poland these happened in 1991. It marked a huge change in the balance of power and the end of Yalta and the Cold War.

This was the best news for Eastern Europe, but for us it had come too late. In 1989, my friends and I were all over sixty-five. Sadly, some of them had died and were buried in England. All our children had been born in England and many of them had their own children. It was too late for us to move back to Poland. It would have meant leaving our children and our grandchildren behind. They had all been born in England, educated there and mostly thought themselves English, of Polish descent. If this wasn't enough, the pre-war borders had not been restored. Eastern Poland remained part of Ukraine, which also gained its independence from the USSR in the same year.

What about my beloved brother, Adam? We had no news of him for years after the end of the war. No news from Poland from anyone who he may have been in touch with or from authorities who may have had lists of victims. In the end, we could only assume that he did indeed perish in Katyń, but in my heart, I pray every day that he is still alive, living a happy life somewhere in safety.

It seemed that almost no one, except those from Eastern Europe, had ever heard of the Katyń genocide. For years the Russians and Germans blamed each other for the atrocity. The British and American Governments did not want to damage relations with their newly formed Russian ally, which meant that the crime was left unsolved.[6] It took a long time before the true identity of those responsible for the massacre was established beyond doubt.

It later became clear that the genocide happened in 1940. At that time, the Russians had occupied the area where the mass graves in the Katyń forest, near Smolensk, were found. The Germans invaded the area at the end of June, 1941. The Russians had previously been asked by the Polish authorities about the thousands of missing officers. They had denied any knowledge of them. If they had known that the Germans had murdered the officers, as they claimed, why did they not say so and free themselves from any blame? But they did not.

If the Germans had committed the atrocity, would they reveal that they had found the graves or would they have kept quiet about the heinous crime? It took many decades and investigations to establish the truth, that the Russians were unequivocally guilty of the genocide, a truth which was covered up for over half a century. [7, 8, 9]

Epilogue

Sussex – England, The Year 2000, Autumn

'Run along now James. Go and play, that's enough for now.'

'Oh Granny, tell me some more, please. I love to hear your stories, *Kochana Babcia*.

In the year 2000, I am out walking on the hills of Sussex, in southern England. I am wrapped in a warm, quilted jacket to ward off the chilly, early autumn air. The golden fields are slowly turning brown as are the trees: a myriad of gold, green and brown shades interwoven across the horizon like plaited silken cords on a thickly woven tapestry rolled out to warm the cooling earth. The sun shines obliquely at this time of year creating a series of its own gently smudged brushstrokes across the landscape. From the top of the Downs, I can clearly see the corn has been harvested and almost all collected in. Only a few, last bales remain in the fields waiting to be brought in.

In a corner of a field, the remnants of a splash of

red poppies, flutter in the distance. The last poppies of September, a symbol of all the lost and fallen in the wars. My heart aches for my parents, for my family, for all the soldiers who died, all the men, women and children: Jadwiga and her newborn, Gabriel, Karoline, who were robbed of their lives, for the victims of the heinous Holocaust and Katyń, for all the families deported to Siberia and to other forgotten places of the Soviet Union and for my dear brother, Adam.

I mourn with all those who have lost loved ones because of the atrocities of this senseless war. What has it achieved? I mourn the estimated seventy million killed.

For those who have survived, a triumph, or a hollow emptiness, filled with hideous and painful memories and feelings of disillusionment and resentment about their lost youth and stolen past? Futures full of hopes changed forever. Wings clipped by the cruel smite of the sword.

I wonder what has become of Alex. Dearest Alex, I love you and always will. You were my first love; you will always have a place in my heart. If only we had met in another time. I waited for you. I hoped and prayed you would come. But how could we ever find each other? I couldn't go back to Bortków and you couldn't come out of the Soviet Union. It was impossible. I remember Juzef, your father, whose kindness to me I will always treasure.

The colour of the poppies is a poignant reminder of a distant past before the ordeal of my teenage years. An unstoppable tear rolls down my cheek, followed by more. I remember the yellow waves of corn when I rode with Papa and lost my hat with its floating red ribbon. Bright red pearl drops of blood flow from the ribbon across the field. Each large drop spreads and merges with another, flooding the whole field and staining it crimson. But Mother comes. She wipes it clean with her smile and tells us a story of love and adventure. The glorious colours of summer return stronger than before. Papa is walking back, smiling and waving at me.

For over the last half a century, England has been my home. Here comes the small figure of a boy who, a few moments earlier ran on ahead across the hills, exploring new paths at every twist and turn. My darling grandson is running back to me.

'*Babcia*, why are you crying?' says the inquisitive eight-year-old.

I put my arm around him.

'Well, my dearest James, when I remember the war and parts of my story, it does make me sad, but my tears turn to tears of joy when I see you. You make me very happy.'

'I love you *Babcia* and I love hearing your story. Please tell me more.' We hug each other tightly. It pleases me, more than he will ever know, that he can say 'Granny' in Polish.

'I hope and pray that you never experience anything like it, my dear child,' I say. He is only eight, so of course, I only tell him some parts.

My thoughts change to feelings of happiness. After all that I have been through and all that has happened, I thank God that I was blessed with Kazimierz, my loving husband and a loving family of my own, and that they want to know my story of survival.

Every day I pray for peace; that nothing like this war will ever happen again.

'Forgive us our trespasses as we forgive those who trespass against us.'[4]

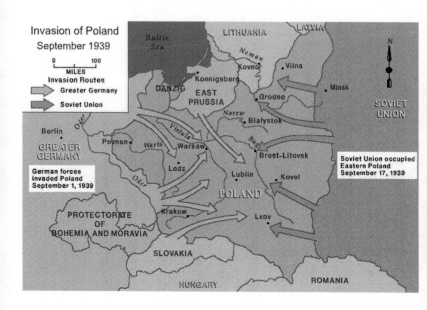

The Invasion of Poland, September 1939

Gdansk
Wilno
(Vilnius)
Bialystok
Nazi-Soviet
pact border
1947 border
Brest
Warszawa
Wroclaw
Kraków
Lwów
(L'viv)
Received by
Poland 1945
Annexed by
Soviet Union 1945
THE CURZON LINE

Poland, the Curzon Line, Pre and Post 1945 Borders of Poland

Footnotes

Part 1
Chapter 1
1. Note on names – Many Polish names have a formal and informal version, eg. Zofia/Zosia, Genowefa/Genia, Jozefa/Juzia (English equivalent: Sophie, Genevieve, Josephine).

Chapter 2
1. Cyprian Norwid, (1821-1883) Polish poet, playwright and artist.
2. Terms 'Polish', 'Poles' throughout the text refer to all ethnic minorities living in pre-war Poland, mostly as citizens of Poland. This includes Jews, Ukrainians, Ruthenians, Lithuanians and others.
3. From Cyprian Norwid, 'My Song' 11.
4. Newspaper Headlines: 1. Le Figaro, 2. Chicago Sunday Tribune, 3. The Journal Times, Racine Wisconsin.

Part 2
Chapter 2
1. NKVD, 'Narodnyi Kommissariat Vnutrennikh Del,' The People's Commissariat of Internal Affairs, the Soviet police and secret police.

Part 3

Chapter 6

1. The headline only is from The San Francisco Chronicle, 24th August, 1939
2. The Journal Times, Racine Wisconsin, 17th September, 1939

Part 4

Chapter 2

1. E. Huntingdon, 'The Unsettled Account,' (1986)

Chapter 4

1. General Szyszko-Bohusz, General of the Polish Army wrote that there needed to be flexibility in the recruitment process. Officially, women aged 18-45 were needed for medical training for the medical battalion, hospital and paramedic work.

Chapter 5

1. N. Davies, 'Trail of Hope,' (Oxford, 2015) The final number evacuated was approximately 114,500.
2. H. Kochanski, 'The Eagle Unbowed, Poland and the Poles in the Second World War,' (London, 2013)
3. H. Kochanski, ibid. Around 4,000 Polish Jewish soldiers were in Anders's Army. 3,000 chose to remain in Palestine. Anders was sympathetic to the choice the Jewish soldiers faced, asserting that it was their right to choose. Among those who remained was Menachem Begin, who later became the 6th Prime Minister of Israel.

Chapter 7

1. Documents on Polish–Soviet Relations, (London, Heinemann 1961), General Sikorski Historical Institute, Volume 1 1939-1943, 523-4
2. A. Paul, 'Katyń: The Untold Story of Stalin's Polish Massacre,' Charles Scribner's Sons, NY, 1991
3. N. Davies, ibid.

Chapter 9

1. Biblical reference, New Testament, Matthew 7:13
2. Z. Wawer, 'General Anders and the Battle for Monte Cassino,' in Pyłat, Ciechanowski & Suchcitz, 'General Władysław Anders: Soldier and Leader of the Free Poles in Exile' (2008)
3. 'Hejnał' – A military trumpet signal dating back to a Tartar attack in the 14th century, in which a bugler was killed by the shot of an arrow to his throat. It is played and interrupted to commemorate the moment of his death.
4. 1,692,000 people. US Congress. House Select Committee on Communist Aggression. 'Communist Takeover and Occupation of Poland.' Special report No.1. 82d US Government Printing Office, 1955.
5. H. Sarner, 'General Anders and the Soldiers of the Second Polish Corps' (Cathedral City, CA, 1977)

Part 5

Chapter 1

1. E. McGilvray, 'The Black Devil's March. A Doomed Odyssey: The 1st Polish Armoured Division 1939-1945,' (Solihull, 2003)

2. Kazimierz Nowak's friends in The First Armoured Regiment during and after the war in England included: Bolesław Grabiec, Stanisław Gudowski, Czesław Jacyna, Tadeusz Soborański, Władysław Szulc, Jan Wosiek, Benjamin Żarkow

3. K. Nowak, 'The Circumstances of the Death of Major M. Bartosiński,' Information Bulletin of the Friends of the First Armoured Regiment, (London, 1979) No.77

4. From 'The Lord's Prayer,' 'Our Father.'

5. The extended family in the UK, some of whom had experienced the Siberian deportation, included: Janina Grabiec, Sabina Gudowska, Hanna Jacyna, Irena Soberańska, Ludmila Szulc, Stefania Wosiek, Zdzisława Żarków and 2 above.

6. After the war, during the cold war period, there would be many attempts to investigate who was responsible for the Katyń crime, but at that time, it was still a delicate period.

7. Anna M. Cienciala, Natalia S. Lebedeva, Wojciech Materski, (eds), 'Katyń: Crime without Punishment,' (London, 2007)

8. In 1992 Boris Yeltsin, President of the Russian Federation, publicly admitted evidence of Russian culpability for the Katyń massacre. See Apologies below 1.

9. W. Materski, 'Now Katyń is the most amply documented Stalinist crime.' 'The Polish Army in the USSR 1941-1942,' (Warsaw 1992), 'Katyń: Documents of Genocide: Documents and Materials from the Soviet Archives turned over to Poland on October 14, 1992,' (Warsaw, 1993)

Afterword

'1,692,000 Poles, including Jews, Ukrainians, White Ruthenians were deported to Russia. This included, in addition to the 250,000 officers and soldiers of the Polish Army, 990,000 civilians taken from their homes and deported because of their 'nationalistic bourgeois background', 250,000 political 'class enemies', 210,000 Poles conscripted in the Soviet Army and sent deep into the USSR, and 12,000 Poles from the Baltic area. Among these deportees were 160,000 children and adolescents.'[1]

The number of survivors of the ordeal was approximately one third of the original 1.692 million. 114,500 evacuees,[2] left the Soviet Union with General Anders across the Caspian Sea. This included 85,000 men and women of the Corps II.[3]

1 US Congress. House Select Committee on Communist Aggression. 'Communist Takeover and Occupation of Poland.' Special Report No.1. 82d US Government Printing Office, 1955
2 N. Davies, 'Trail of Hope,' (Oxford, 2015)
3 Halik Kochanski, 'The Eagle Unbowed,' (London, 2013)

General Władysław Anders lived in London after the war. He was a key member of the Polish Government in Exile in London. He died in 1970, aged 77 and is buried at the Polish War Cemetery, Monte Cassino among soldiers from the Corps II, according to his wishes.

Genia, Wojtek and their children settled in Toronto, Canada. Jozefa, Lucia and Antoni all married and had eight children between them. Lucia is the sole survivor from the original group at the time of writing. She lives in Canada to this day and has great grandchildren. Leon and Kazik married and lived with their families in Boston and London respectively. Adam was never traced.

By the beginning of the new Millennium, Zosia had lived in London, England for over half a century. She died in 2017, just short of her 94th birthday, having spent seventy-one years in England and only the first fifteen years of her life in Poland. The deportation, journey back to Europe and arrival in Britain, covering a distance of more than nine thousand miles, lasted over seven years. Her husband, Kazimierz died in 1995, aged 81. They were married for forty-six years and are survived by children and grandchildren.

Apologies

1. In 1992, Boris Yeltsin, President of the Russian Federation, publicly admitted evidence of Russian culpability for the Katyń massacre of over 14,500 Polish officers and civilians. In 1995 he accepted responsibility in a letter to the Polish Prime Minister.

2. In September 2003, Prime Minister Tony Blair apologised for the British Government not inviting the Polish allied forces to the WWII Victory Parade in 1946 in London. The purpose of the omission was seen to be to avoid antagonising the new Russian ally. To make up for this, Polish veterans were invited to lead the sixtieth anniversary parade in July 2005.

3. In 2005, on the sixtieth anniversary of the end of WWII, President George W Bush apologised for the outcome of the Yalta conference in 1945, saying:

'The captivities of millions in central and eastern Europe will be remembered as one of the greatest wrongs of history.'

Acknowledgements

To the writers listed in the footnotes, my sincere indebtedness for their detailed and enlightening documentation which has been crucial in filling in the historical gaps. In particular, to the 'Mémoires, 1939-1946' of General Władysław Anders, to Norman Davies's, 'Trail of Hope' and Halik Kochanski's scholarly, 'The Eagle Unbowed, Poland and the Poles in the Second World War.'

To Bryden, my husband and my son, James, my thanks for their unfailing interest and support over the last few years.

Most of all, thanks must go to my mother, Zofia for keeping her story alive by telling me what happened to her and her family during the Second World War. Thanks also to my father, Kazimierz for recounting his experiences. It is the story of the destruction, displacement and exile they lived through as a result of war.

End note

After World War II Lwów, which had been in Poland before the war, became Lviv in Ukraine. Zofia's home village of Bortków became Bortkiv in Ukraine. All of eastern Poland became part of the USSR.

History does indeed repeat itself. There are parallels between events which happened in Poland during and after WWII and the events, over eighty years later, in Ukraine in 2022.

 **Matador**

For exclusive discounts on Matador titles,
sign up to our occasional newsletter at
troubador.co.uk/bookshop